There was nothing elegant about their kiss.

He flattened her lips against her teeth, flatly insisted that she acknowledge and react to him. Her mouth was ripe and juicy, and he devoured her hungrily, sucking in the taste of her, drawing her to him until she became a part of him. He'd love to gentle the kiss, to savor the rich taste of her, to enjoy her languidly and completely.

But first, he wanted all of her—no reservations. He felt the piece she was holding back. It dangled tantalizingly, just beyond his reach. But he also felt her control of that piece of herself slipping….

Dear Reader,

Please allow me to take this opportunity to thank the hundreds of you who have contacted me over the past two years to ask about Kat's story. Without your encouragement, I'm not sure I'd ever have found this story, let alone written it. So this one's for you.

That said, it's a thrill for me to welcome you to Kat's book! It might have been a long time in the cooking, but I'd like to think the meal was worth the wait. The Medusas are back in action, this time on the beautiful island of Barbados.

It was the appearance of Jeff Steiger, the one man with exactly what it would take to sweep Kat off her feet, that gave me my inspiration. As soon as he waltzed across my mind with his killer dimples and irresistible New Orleans drawl, I knew Kat was sunk. It's not often that a Medusa owes a man for much of anything, but in this case, Kat owes him one. For without him, *Medusa's Master* might not have taken shape.

So buckle your seat belt, hang on tight, and get ready to rock and roll as Kat and Jeff sweep you away on the latest wild ride of the Medusas!

Cindy

CINDY DEES

Medusa's Master

Silhouette®

Romantic

SUSPENSE

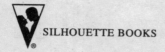 SILHOUETTE BOOKS

Recycling programs for this product may not exist in your area.

ISBN-13: 978-0-373-27640-0

MEDUSA'S MASTER

Books by Cindy Dees

Silhouette Romantic Suspense

Behind Enemy Lines #1176
Line of Fire #1253
A Gentleman and a Soldier #1307
Her Secret Agent Man #1353
Her Enemy Protector #1417
The Lost Prince #1441
†*The Medusa Affair* #1477
†*The Medusa Seduction* #1494
**The Dark Side of Night #1509
Killer Affair #1524
**Night Rescuer #1561
The 9-Month Bodyguard #1564
**Medusa's Master #1570

Silhouette Bombshell

Killer Instinct #16
†*The Medusa Project* #31
Target #42
†*Medusa Rising* #60
†*The Medusa Game* #79
Haunted Echoes #101
†*The Medusa Prophecy* #122

*Charlie Squad
†The Medusa Project
**H.O.T. Watch

CINDY DEES

started flying airplanes while sitting in her dad's lap at the age of three and got a pilot's license before she got a driver's license. At age fifteen, she dropped out of high school and left the horse farm in Michigan where she grew up to attend the University of Michigan.

After earning a degree in Russian and East European Studies, she joined the U.S. Air Force and became the youngest female pilot in its history. She flew supersonic jets, VIP airlift and the C-5 Galaxy, the world's largest airplane. She also worked part-time gathering intelligence. During her military career, she traveled to forty countries on five continents, was detained by the KGB and East German secret police, got shot at, flew in the first Gulf War, met her husband and amassed a lifetime's worth of war stories.

Her hobbies include professional Middle Eastern dancing, Japanese gardening and medieval reenacting. She started writing on a one-dollar bet with her mother and was thrilled to win that bet with the publication of her first book in 2001. She loves to hear from readers and can be contacted at www.cindydees.com.

This book is dedicated to you. Yes, you.

Without you and all of the other wonderful and loyal readers who have supported the Medusas over the past five years, this series would have died off long ago. But because of you, the snake ladies live on, we all get to keep playing in their awesome world. Thanks from the bottom of my heart.

To all of the wonderful readers who have supported the Medusas over the past five years and kept them going strong through thick and thin.

Chapter 1

Katrina Kim stepped out into the cavernous H.O.T. Watch headquarters, gazing around in shock as much at the banks of computers and analysts as at the domed enormity of the cave enclosing it all in perpetual night. And she'd thought the mini-submarine ride to get to the inside of this hollowed-out volcano had been wild. This place was *incredible*.

"Ahh, there you are, Captain Kim." An attractive woman wearing khaki shorts and a dark polo shirt strode toward her, holding out her hand. "I'm Jennifer Blackfoot."

Katrina studied the offered hand impassively. A grab and twist at the base of the thumb would put the woman down on the ground. Or, there was the pressure point in the wrist, which would bring a grown man in a full battle rage to a screeching halt. Or there was always the tried-and-true bend-and-snap to break fingers and generally maim the sensitive instrument that was the human hand.

Gently, she clasped the woman's proffered hand. "Please.

Call me Kat." Standard protocol to ask civilians to use her first name. It put them at ease around Special Forces operatives like her.

Kat was one of the founding members of the Medusas, the first all-female Special Forces team the U.S. military had fielded a couple of years earlier. The Medusas had long since earned their battle stripes and were well respected within the Special Forces community. At the moment, the Medusas were in North Carolina on call, waiting for a crisis to blow up somewhere that required their particular brand of attention. In another month, all the Medusas were scheduled to stand down and go into a training cycle. In the meantime, she'd been sent to this classified facility in the Caribbean on a special assignment.

She didn't know anything about the mission. She'd been awakened by a phone call early this morning, telling her to be at the airfield in an hour in civilian clothes with warm-weather gear for immediate deployment. And here she was, none the wiser as to what would be expected of her, knowing only that it would be extremely high risk. Otherwise, they wouldn't have called her.

God, she loved this job.

Suppressing an actual smile of enjoyment at the low-level hum of adrenaline coursing through her veins, she glanced over at the civilian woman walking beside her and asked, "When will I receive my mission briefing?"

Her guide looked over, surprised. "General Wittenauer didn't fill you in?"

"No, ma'am."

The woman laughed. "Don't 'ma'am' me. I'm just a civilian. My friends call me Jennifer or Jenn."

Kat pursed her lips. She rarely stuck around anywhere long enough to make actual friends. "The way I hear it, you run this outfit."

Jennifer shrugged. "I run the civilian side of the house.

Commander Hathaway runs the military side. Frankly, being in charge around here mostly consists of sprinting like crazy to stay at the front of the stampede."

Kat nodded knowingly. Although they all tried to impose as much order as possible on their world, Special Ops was often a chaotic enterprise.

Jennifer ushered her through a thick, steel door and into a low, long corridor hewn out of rough rock. "You'll be working with Jeff Steiger. His handle's Maverick. He'll bring you up to speed on his little project."

A little project, huh? An odd choice of words for a Special Ops mission.

Jennifer pulled out a cell phone and made a call. "This is Raven. Where's Maverick?" A short pause. "Thanks."

Raven? A good handle for the woman. She had long, black hair that formed a shimmering, silken fall almost to her hips.

"Captain Steiger is in the gym."

"There's a gym down here?" Kat asked, surprised.

"We've got it all. Cafeteria, sleeping quarters, long-term food supplies…there's even a small infirmary."

Impressive. She followed Jennifer-Raven through a labyrinth of hallways to yet another anonymous door. If this place were ever invaded, she wished the intruders luck finding anything. Nothing was marked in this maze, and every hall, every door, looked exactly the same.

As they stepped into a well-outfitted gym, her companion announced, "Ladies' locker room is behind the weight machines. You'll probably find Maverick on the fighting mats pummeling some poor sod. I saw on the training schedule that he and his Ops team were going to be practicing unarmed combat this afternoon."

"Is he good?" Kat murmured.

"He's unofficial champ of the entire bunker. And we've got upwards of sixty operators attached to this outfit."

Interesting. It had been a long time since anyone had given

her a real challenge in unarmed combat. Oh, she faked having to struggle against most guys, but she usually held back. It was for the best that way.

Jennifer made her farewells, and Kat looked around. It smelled like every other gym in creation, of sweat and disinfectant, burnt rubber and iron. Weights clanked on the far side of a currently empty basketball court, and off to her right, a group of men made the distinctive shouted grunts of martial artists in training. Hidoshi-san, the man who'd adopted her and had been father, teacher and sensei to her from infancy, had called the shouts *kiais*, but each martial school had its own name for them.

She strolled across the hardwood basketball floor, observing a half-dozen pairs of men wrestling around on the mat, practicing ground-fighting techniques. It looked like a Brazilian jiujitsu variant they were doing, with some of the usual rules suspended to modify it for urban combat.

BJJ was a twentieth-century variant on a much older form of judo. Mentally she turned her nose up at it. Her training had been in the original, classical traditions from one of the great modern masters: judo—the way of grappling, karate-do—the way of the open hand, kendo—the way of the sword, iai-do—the way of the fast sword, even aikido—the way of harmony.

The men's movements looked jerky and forced as they moved through joint locking and choking exercises. However, in a real fight, it wasn't about beauty. It was all about putting the other guy down before he put you down.

She set down her gear bags and rifle case to watch. The men finished the sequence and climbed to their feet, breathing hard. They began to spar in a standing position, trading kicks and punches.

One of the men, a good-looking guy with blond-streaked hair and a surfer's tan, glanced over at her, then did a double take. His partner took the opportunity to clock him with a fast kick to the side of the head. Surfer guy went down like a ton of bricks.

She bit back a smile at his expense. That had to have hurt. He rolled onto his back and executed a nifty back-arch and flip that landed him on his feet. Showboating for her, no doubt. The move took stomach strength and looked good in the movies, but was impractical in most actual fights. Any half-decent ground fighter would never give you a chance to get back to your feet at all, let alone in so flashy a fashion.

She studied surfer guy as he swaggered over to her. Strong. Lean. Fit. Lacking in flexibility if she had to guess. And in subtlety, for that matter. The grinning leer in his gaze was beyond obvious. According to her Eastern upbringing, it bordered on insulting. In the West, it was a mild flirtation. She sighed. Yet again, her two worlds collided. She had to admit, though, he was cute. No, strike cute. He was hot.

"Hey, baby. Y'all new in town?" he drawled with a hint of New Orleans in his voice.

"You're not talking to me, are you?" she replied smoothly. "Because I don't recall giving you permission to call me that."

"Whatchya gonna do about it…baby?" Were it not for the utterly charming grin and devastating dimples that accompanied the comment, she'd have flattened him on the spot. As it was, she stepped forward politely and held out her hand.

"My name's Katrina Kim—"

He smiled triumphantly over his shoulder at the other men, who'd all stopped sparring to stare at her. Still grinning confidently, he took her hand.

In a flash, she spun and yanked, twisting the guy's entire arm and flipping him neatly over her hip. He slammed heavily to the floor. Before his bulk had hardly finished smacking the mat face-first, she pounced, kneeling on his neck with her knee and yanking his arm up and back uncomfortably behind him.

"—and don't call me baby," she finished coolly. Inside, she churned. She *hated* being forced into having to reveal a glimpse of her martial arts skills. Hidoshi had always considered it a grave failure of *Shin,* the Mind, to be forced into using violence. But sometimes a girl had to do what a girl had to do.

The other men gaped, equal parts stunned and appalled.

Without letting the man on the floor go, she asked them pleasantly, "Is one of you Captain Steiger? I was told I might find him here."

The guy beneath her lurched, and she gave a sharp jerk on his arm, effectively and completely subduing him. Grins were beginning to spread across the other men's faces.

One of the men answered gravely, "You're standing on him, ma'am."

A thoroughly unladylike curse shot through her head. Great. She'd just taken down and humiliated the man she was supposed to work for on this mission. Why was it the Medusas always seemed to get off to a rocky start with the men they worked with? She sighed. At least she and the good captain had established that she didn't like being called baby. It was probably handy to have gotten that out of the way, at any rate.

Lying facedown on the floor, Jeff Steiger tried wiggling something small—he started with his pinkie finger. Mistake. Pain shot down his arm and exploded in his shoulder. Man. So much for impressing the hot chick in the gym. She was a little thing, not particularly heavy kneeling on his neck, but damned if she didn't have him tied up practically in a pretzel.

Thankfully, she released his arm and let him up without him actually having to cry uncle. He climbed painfully to his feet, eyeing the young woman warily.

As if it wasn't bad enough that she'd taken him down, she

was also a drop-dead eyeful. Exotic, definitely part Asian. Maybe Korean. Her features were refined. Delicate even. But that grip on his hand had been pure steel, and the strength behind it that had put him on the ground had been shocking.

He smiled at her ruefully. "How 'bout we start over? My name's Jeff Steiger. But you can call me Maverick if you like." Putting on his best Sunday church manners, he added, "It's a pleasure to meet you, ma'am."

She nodded briefly.

"You said you were looking for me?"

She frowned, and even that was a delicate thing, her finely drawn eyebrows arching together over an elegant nose. Her eyes were a clear, sweet tea brown.

"General Wittenauer sent me to work with you."

Wittenauer? The Old Man himself? He was the commander-in-chief of the entire Joint Special Operations Command. Jeff had sent a request up channels for a Special Forces operator who was unusually agile and had expertise in electronics. Why in the hell had the general sent down this girl instead?

Jeff cursed under his breath. It could only mean one thing. Wittenauer thought his theory on the robberies was a load of bull. He hadn't even taken Jeff's report seriously enough to send him a real operator, let alone the one he needed.

He realized the girl was staring at him expectantly. He mumbled, "Uh, sorry. Did the general send me a message or something?"

"No. Just me."

What the hell? "If you'll pardon my bluntness, who are you?"

She lifted an eyebrow at that. "Captain Katrina Kim. U.S. Army. Joint Special Operations Command, Medusa Project. Sniper, linguist, electronics and black ops specialist."

He stared. He didn't even know where to begin reacting to that mouthful. Her? A sniper? *No way.* Black Ops? *Get out.* Finally, he sputtered, "What the hell is the Medusa Project? Never heard of it."

She pursed her mouth into a Kewpie-doll pout and said mildly, "You must not have a high enough security clearance to have heard of it."

"Are you dissing my security clearances?" Indignation started low in his gut. "I'll have you know the *name* of my security clearance is classified, lady."

Somehow, even with her face completely devoid of expression and her body utterly still, she managed to convey complete disdain for him and his clearance.

"What the hell kind of clearances do you have?" he challenged.

She shrugged. "I'm allowed to carry firearms in the presence of the president of the United States."

Jeez. He was familiar with such a clearance, and they didn't come much higher than that. "And have you ever been armed in the presence of the president?"

She answered evenly. "Several times. He awarded me my first combat medal."

Who in the hell was *this lady?*

"Perhaps we can go somewhere more…private…to talk?" she suggested.

He glanced over his shoulder at their avid audience. "My guys are okay. They're all operators, complete with fancy security clearances. They won't tell tales."

One of them piped up drolly. "But we're bloody well telling everyone in the bunker that an itty bitty thing in a skirt tossed your happy butt on the floor."

Jeff scowled. Damn. There went his reputation. To the itty bitty thing in a skirt in question, he said, "Let me clean up. And then we can go to my office and talk."

She was waiting for him when he emerged from the locker room five minutes later. He'd intended to take a long, hot shower and make her wait, but inexplicable curiosity, eagerness even, to learn more about her had turned his shower into a hasty affair lasting barely two minutes.

"May I take your bags for you?" he offered, startled at how bulky and heavy they looked now that he paid attention to them. She didn't seem fazed by them, though.

"No, thank you. The Medusas make a policy of hauling their own gear."

They stepped out into the hallway and he turned toward his temporary digs in an underground warehouse space that he'd appropriated a few weeks back.

"What exactly are the Medusas?" he asked as they walked.

"'Who are they?' is the appropriate question."

Not real chatty, this self-contained woman. When she didn't continue, he said, "Okay, then. Who are they?"

"Special Forces team. All-female."

"All—*what?*" Female? No. Freaking. Way. There was *no way* women could do the job he and his buddies did. None. Not possible.

She didn't bother to reply. Apparently, she figured he'd heard her correctly the first time.

She might not let him carry her bags for her, but he did open the door for her when they arrived at his office. She nodded her thanks as she stepped inside. The true black of underground shrouded the room, and she paused in the thin shaft of light spilling weakly into the space from behind them. He reached out and flipped the wall switch beside the door. Halogen lights flashed on overhead, illuminating the cavernous space.

His companion studied the elaborate mock-ups of walls, and partial rooms scattered all over the spacious room, looking like stored television show sets. He closed the door behind them. "Welcome to my laboratory."

"What are you researching?"

"The appropriate question is 'Who is the Ghost?'"

"Okay. Who is the Ghost?"

"Our mission. Yours and mine."

"Come again?"

He smiled at the incongruousness of such a quintessentially military phrase issuing from her quintessentially feminine mouth.

"The Ghost. We'll talk more about him later if it turns out you can actually help me. My desk is over here." He led her to a glass-enclosed space tucked in one corner of the storage area.

He led her inside and moved behind his desk to sit down. He actually felt safer with the bulky piece between them. She'd taken him by surprise with that throw of hers. Next time, though, he'd be ready for the move. "I'm afraid I need you to tell me a little more about yourself before I can bring you on board this project."

"Captain Steiger, I am an experienced and decorated Special Forces operative, and General Wittenauer thinks I'm the right person to help you with whatever you're doing. This isn't a job interview. It's a done deal; I have been assigned to this mission."

He studied her, frustrated. What the hell was he supposed to do with a girl? What on God's green Earth was the Old Man up to?

He must've muttered that last question aloud, because Captain Kim replied dryly, "I don't speak for General Wittenauer. Why don't you call him and ask?"

His eyes narrowed. He could smell a bluff at a hundred paces. Fine. He picked up the phone. "Hey, Carter, get me JSOC headquarters, will ya?" He'd show her a thing or two about playing poker with a good ol' boy.

The familiar voice of Mary Norton, General Wittenauer's personal secretary, came on the line. Jeff drawled, "Well, hey there, Ms. Mary. How's my favorite lady in the whole world doing today?"

The secretary's formal tone thawed considerably. "I'm fine, Captain Steiger. And what can I do for you?"

"Is the Old—is General Wittenauer available?"

The secretary laughed. "Yes. The Old Man's here. He's only in his early fifties, you know. One moment."

A brusque voice said, "Go."

"Sir. This is Captain Steiger down at H.O.T. Watch. I'm calling about the operative I asked for to help me catch the Ghost."

"Hasn't she arrived yet? Her plane must've gotten held up."

Her. He'd said *her.* The woman sitting before him wasn't a mistake. Sonofa—

"She's a hell of an operator, Jeff. Just the ticket for what you need."

"But I need a combat operator. Someone to catch a thief—"

The general cut him off. "And that's why I sent you Cobra. If anyone can get the job done, it's her. Trust me, Steiger. She's a pro."

Cobra? She had a field handle? Great. Some chick with delusions of being one of the boys.

"Let me know how your experiment goes, son. We've got some very high-powered folks breathing down the necks of their congressmen, and that sort of crap rolls downhill fast. It's landing on me deep and still steaming over here at the Pentagon."

"Yes, sir. I will, sir." He hung up the phone, staring at it stonily.

A melodic voice interrupted his dark musings. "We're going to catch a thief, are we? What's he stealing?"

"Art."

"What kind of art?"

"Paintings. The cheapest one so far has a price tag in the two million dollar range."

"Where are these paintings being stolen from?"

He looked up at her grimly. Wittenauer wanted him to give the girl a try? Then that's just what he'd do. "Come with me."

He led her out into the larger room and over to one of the full-room mock-ups. He stopped in the doorway of the two-story-high structure. He flipped a switch, and a labyrinth of red laser beams cut across the space. He pointed to a window on his left.

"Come in through that. Don't touch the floor. Cross the room to that painting over there." He pointed at a poster-size print of a buxom blonde in a skimpy, wet bikini, hanging on the far wall.

Kat commented dryly, "The little known follow-up portrait to the Mona Lisa? The Moaning Lay-me?"

He grinned reluctantly. "That Da Vinci dude was sure 'nuff a fellow of fine taste."

Kat eyed the mock-up assessingly. "What equipment may I use?"

"Whatever you want. I've got climbing cups, rope, grappling hooks, crampons, you name it." He gestured at a pile of gear on a table just outside the door.

"I'll need to change my clothes."

"Fine."

"Where?"

He jerked a thumb over his shoulder. "My office. I won't look."

She shrugged. "My lingerie covers more than that girl's bikini."

"Too bad," he quipped. A twinge in his shoulder from his earlier fall kept him from saying more. She might not catch him by surprise again, but he didn't relish a straight-up fight with her. After all, he had a rule against hitting girls. Yup, that was why he didn't want to tangle with her, he told himself firmly.

She emerged from his office in a one-piece gray bodysuit that made him about swallow his tongue. Whoa. She was *perfect*. She had curves in all the right places, was slender in all the right places. She was a tiny little thing. No more than five foot three. Though slim, definite muscles flexed beneath her sea-land suit.

The high-tech gray fabric was waterproof when submerged, but when dry, it breathed like cloth and allowed the wearer to sweat normally, unlike the neoprene suits divers traditionally wore.

While he struggled not to stare, she moved to the pile of equipment and confidently sorted through it, slinging climbing ropes over her shoulders and strapping on a climbing harness. She clipped carabiners and belaying devices on to her waist belt and quickly strapped a knife to her thigh. She certainly handled the gear like she knew what to do with it.

She asked, "Have you got three or four handheld, signaling mirrors?"

"Coming up." He went over to an equipment locker and pulled them out.

She held out her hand without even looking over at him. The mirrors disappeared into one of her waist pouches. She walked over to the "outside" of the window.

"Does noise matter?"

"Not for today's purposes."

"Time limit?"

"Not this time."

She leaped up onto the window ledge as lightly as her feline namesake and balanced there easily. He watched with interest as she threaded a spare radio antenna through the sighting hole in the middle of one of the mirrors. She broke off the end of the antenna and poked its now sharp end into the drywall above her head. A slight adjustment, and the mirror caught one of the laser signals and reflected it away from the space above the window. She repeated the process until she'd created a gap in the net of lasers. Clever.

She ran a stud finder across the wall above the window until it flashed green and beeped. Quickly, she reached up and hammered in a crampon. She slapped on a carabiner and ran the end of her nylon webbing rope through it. With surprising upper-body strength for a woman, she pulled herself up a couple of feet and tied off her harness.

She repeated the whole process until she'd reached the ceiling. The laser beams stopped about four feet shy of the ceiling. Bemused, he watched her pull out some sort of climbing cleats that hadn't come from his pile of gear and buckle them to her feet and hands.

His jaw dropped as she struck the ceiling hard to sink her cleats into it, and commenced crawling, spiderlike, across the surface. How she clung upside down like that and didn't fall, he had no idea. He'd never seen anything like it. In three minutes or so, she'd reached the far wall. She planted a crampon, tied off a rope and shimmied down it quickly, using her mirrors to deflect the lasers.

"You want me to take the picture, or just draw a mustache and horns on it?" she asked casually, spinning gently in her harness next to the poster.

Damn. She didn't even sound out of breath!

"Whatever you do, don't defile Bambi. She's an icon around here."

"Do you need me to retrace my route, or have you seen enough?"

"That's enough." He tried to sound unaffected, but he'd never seen anything like what she'd just done. The strength it took to cling to a ceiling like that boggled his mind. She must have a crazy strength-to-weight ratio.

Well, why not? He'd predicted that the Ghost had a similar strength-to-weight ratio. It was the only way to explain some of the climbing the guy had to have done to successfully steal the paintings he had. Jeff just hadn't expected to encounter the same sort of strength in a woman.

Kat efficiently retrieved her climbing gear and lowered herself to the floor. She walked toward him, winding her climbing rope around her left arm as she came. "Any more hoops you want me to jump through before you believe who I am?" she asked, looking him dead in the eye.

Without ever taking his eyes off hers, he reached for the holster at his right hip lightning fast and quick drew his pistol, whipping it out to point it at her.

Chapter 2

Kat had a split second to react to the weapon. She had two choices: aggression or evasion. He was a Special Forces operator—the gun *would* be loaded and the safety off. She opted for both responses. She dodged low and across his body from the gun, and then launched herself upward. Like most shooters, he'd turned his gun shoulder forward slightly, which threw him slightly off balance. She slammed her body into him to accentuate his balance problem. A quick hook with her ankle, a karate thrust with the heel of her hand to his shoulder, and he spun to the ground, his gun arm trapped underneath him.

He made a credible grab for her in the jiujitsu style, but she ducked and slipped the grappling hold. This time she rolled him swiftly to his back and straddled his chest. She wanted to look him in the eye when she told him to cut out the martial arts crap. To that end, she maintained a simple thumb hold on him. It was enough to control him if he got any crazy ideas, but it wasn't as psychologically overwhelming as the armlock she'd put on him earlier.

He relaxed beneath her legs. She glared down at him and…and her thoughts derailed completely. Wow. Now those were *blue* eyes. A bright cobalt color lifted straight from the Caribbean Sea.

His mouth curved up into a disarming smile. "I can't believe it took pulling a gun to get you to show your true feelings for me, darlin'."

She leaned back on her heels, which put most of her weight on his stomach. His abdominal muscles contracted into a hard washboard beneath her rear end, supporting her body weight easily. *Yowza.* It was a struggle to maintain her usual even expression.

"Are you done pulling stupid stunts on me, Captain Steiger, or am I out of here?"

His grinned widened. "Depends on how you define stupid."

She arched an eyebrow and replied dryly, "Are you sure you want me to respond to that remark? I'm not sure your ego could take it."

"Ouch. No wonder they call you Cobra. The lady has fangs."

She shrugged. "I thought it was because I spit so well."

Startled laughter escaped him. "How 'bout I put down the cap gun and you let me up off the playground before the other kids start calling me a sissy? As a show of good faith, I'll go first."

She watched impassively as he laid the pistol down by her left knee and slowly lifted his hand away from it. She released his other thumb, her senses on high alert.

She leaned forward, preparatory to climbing off him, when he murmured, "Where are you going? I kinda like you like this."

It wasn't his words that froze her in place. It was the low

purr of his voice, sliding roughly over her skin, no longer boyish but suddenly all man. Or perhaps it was the explosion of…something…low in her belly in response to that black velvet tone of voice.

Her gaze lifted to his in shock. Blue met brown. And to his credit, he didn't smirk at her. In fact, he looked nearly as stunned as she did. They stared deeply at one another for an eternity. Instinctive recognition flared between them. If she didn't know better, she'd say they'd met before. Been passionate lovers in some previous place and time.

"Little Kitty Kat," he crooned.

Shock exploded in her. How did he know that was what Hidoshi called her in his rare affectionate moments? He couldn't possibly… It was just coincidence…but a superstitious chill shivered through her, nonetheless.

His big hands moved slowly—smart man—and came to rest on the tops of her thighs, by her hips. Through the thin fabric of her bodysuit, his palms scalded her.

"Don't go," he murmured, half order, half plea.

"What's happening?" she breathed.

"Don't you know?"

She shook her head, wide-eyed.

"Grandmère called it Cupid's Bolt."

She frowned. Sometimes she felt at a real disadvantage with American slang. Having spent her childhood abroad, she often missed pop-culture references. "I'm sorry—what?"

The last thing she expected entered his brilliant gaze. Unmistakable tenderness. He replied softly, "Cupid's Bolt. It's when you meet someone and it feels like you've been gobsmacked by a big ol' bolt of lighting. Grandmère says it doesn't happen to many folks. But to a lucky few…"

"What happens?" Kat prompted when he didn't continue.

He shrugged. "Game over. True love. Soul mates. Till death do us part."

She was so stunned her jaw actually sagged open.

"We've been struck by Cupid's Bolt, darlin'. It's inevitable. You and me. Get used to it."

"You're telling me we shared a look, and you've declared me your future…what?…sex kitten?"

He laughed. "That doesn't begin to cover it."

Panic threatened to creep into her voice. She managed to force it down, but it was a close call. "What then? Wife? Mother of your children? Soul mate? That's absurd. I'm not even in the market for a relationship, let alone that other stuff."

"Glad to hear it because you're plumb off the market, effective now. You're mine."

"Oh, puh-lease."

He grinned up at her. "I get dibs on telling you I told you so."

He was positively out of his mind. Sure, a tiny part of her twittered like some green girl at how romantic the whole notion was. And he certainly was easy on the eye. But soul mates? Happily ever after? So not in the cards for her.

Long ago she'd dedicated her life to a principle, *junjo-do*, the way of the pure heart. She hadn't dedicated part of her life to that way. She'd dedicated her entire self to the pursuit.

He shrugged philosophically, causing movement between her thighs that drew her attention sharply and completely. His voice was dead serious. "You wait and see. That was Cupid's Bolt, or my name's not Jefferson Delacroix Steiger."

Desperate to lighten the mood and distract him, she quipped, "Delacroix? Did your parents hate you?"

He grinned. Better. Although, man, that thousand-watt smile went right through her. She became aware of his thumbs rubbing absent circles on her legs, straying disturbingly near the sensitive flesh of her inner thighs. She was torn as to whether to ignore it or call attention to it by asking him to stop.

"Delacroix is my mother's maiden name. Our firstborn can

have your maiden name, if you like. Although with a name like Kim, I sure hope it's a girl. I'd hate to stick our son with Kim for a middle name."

"Our—" She was speechless. He was already naming their children? He was certifiable!

He continued blithely, "I suppose growing up with a name like that would help a boy develop character, though."

"Or a hell of a right hook," she added wryly.

Jeff nodded gravely. "If you teach him to fight, he'll have nothing to worry about on that score."

She couldn't help it. She laughed. This was the craziest conversation she'd ever had while sitting on someone's chest. "You're nuts."

She rocked onto the balls of her feet and stood up. She stepped aside lightly and held a hand down to him to help him up. He was tall enough—and she was short enough—that he didn't have to sit all the way up to grasp her hand. He gave a swift yank, and before she knew it, she was sprawled on her stomach across his big body, her face inches from him.

"See, I knew you'd fall for me sooner or later," he murmured.

Oh, my. He smelled good. "Let me up," she demanded.

"Gotta say please. It's important to teach our kids good manners, you know. And we have to set the example for them."

She contemplated fighting him for her freedom, but in this position, his strength would work to her disadvantage. Part of being a warrior of the way was knowing when to back down, too. She sighed. "Pretty please?"

"Pretty, am I?" His voice dropped to a whisper. "You're pretty, too. Beyond pretty. Perfect, in fact."

He thought she was perfect? A rush of warmth shot through her before she knew what had hit her. Then hard, cold reality set in. It didn't matter what he thought of her. They were coworkers. Colleagues. Professional acquaintances. Nothing more. And she had neither the time nor the inclination to allow a man into her life.

His hand, splayed intimately on her lower back, began moving in small, slow circles, expertly massaging away her tension. Her entire lower body turned to jelly right there on the spot. Oh, Lord, that felt good. Coworkers, darn it!

She stiffened reluctantly.

He sighed. "Okay, baby. We can go back to work. For now. But tonight, I'm taking you out for a romantic, candlelit dinner."

He turned her loose without warning. His magic touch was gone, and she felt...bereft.

What in the *hell* was he doing to her?

Jeff climbed cautiously to his feet, watching the woman who'd not once but twice dropped him with an ease that was breathtaking. This tiny little thing—she didn't even reach his chin, for crying out loud—had absolutely manhandled him. Of course, maybe he was just so damned distracted by her he wasn't thinking straight. But, Cupid's Bolt or not, he had a hard time believing that decades of finely honed fighting skills had deserted him at the sight of a pretty face.

Although, pretty didn't quite cover it. She was mesmerizing. He couldn't take his eyes off her. Everything about her was as he'd declared. Perfect. Her skin was flawless—all shades of ivory and cherry blossom pink. Her glossy, black hair was smoothed back into a ponytail with not a single hair daring to stray out of place. And her body—in that wet-dry suit, not a whole hell of a lot was left to the imagination, and every inch of it was exquisite.

To his consternation, she took the chair across from his desk in the gray suit and seemed in no great hurry to get out of it. Maybe she knew the effect it had on him and was using it to throw him off balance. It was working, whether she intended it or not.

He opened the file sitting in the middle of his desk. He didn't actually need it; he knew every fact in it by heart. But it gave him something to look at other than her hypnotic beauty. He cleared his throat. Work. Concentrate on work. "A string of robberies have taken place over the past several months in Barbados along a stretch of real estate known as the Golden Mile. Are you familiar with it?"

"No."

Her voice reminded him of wind chimes. Work, dammit. "It's a string of mega-mansion getaways for the super-rich, lining several beachfront miles. A who's who of the world's richest people own these places. And that leads to a healthy dose of one-upmanship in the homes and their decorations."

A faint smile flickered in her eyes, but her features otherwise remained impassive. So self-contained, she was. Made him wonder what was going on behind that still façade of hers.

"Recently, it has become the vogue to cram these winter hideaways with art. But not just any art. The most expensive art the collectors can find and flaunt."

She replied, "And now this collection has attracted the finest art thieves the world has to offer. Don't these places have pretty outrageous security? The owners can afford it."

Intelligent. She'd already made the next logical leap ahead of his narrative. He nodded. "Go on. Continue your line of thought."

"The U.S. government has been asked to help catch this guy. Which means the local police have failed. I'd guess some influential Americans have been robbed, and they're raising a stink with their congressmen golfing buddies. In a smashing display of not understanding the limitations under which various government agencies operate, said congressmen have had their aides call the FBI, who threw up their hands and declared it outside their jurisdiction. Compounding their blunder, the aides called the CIA and possibly even Interpol. Eventually, their complaints ended up in the Pentagon's lap, and the whole mess has rolled downhill and landed on your desk."

He leaned back in his chair, studying her intently. "That's so accurate it's frightening."

She shrugged. "I've been in the Spec Ops community a while. I've seen a few ops get hosed from above."

He grimaced and didn't bother to reply. They both knew precisely what she was talking about. The bane of the Special Forces world—bureaucratic intervention from desk jockeys thousands of miles from the field of battle.

She looked him square in the eye. "So why am I here? What do you need from me?"

The corner of his mouth quirked up. He answered dryly, "The possible answers to that question beggar the mind. Let's start by reviewing the robberies. I have a few theories about how our thief is pulling off the jobs, but I'd like to hear your thoughts before I share mine."

They put their heads together over all the information he'd painstakingly gathered: police reports, blueprints of homes, schematics of security systems. It took them several hours to sort through all the data. Kat didn't say much. She asked occasional questions, but mostly she just absorbed it all. He dumped a ton of information on her, yet several times near the end, she asked pointed questions about details he'd mentioned briefly, hours earlier. Yup, definitely some extra chocolate chips in this smart cookie.

Finally, she leaned back, staring at nothing in particular. He could all but hear her mind humming as she processed the briefing. He didn't disturb her. Besides, it gave him a chance to study Kat more closely.

She had small ears. Her fingernails were almond shaped, done in one of those pink-and-white manicures. Her skin was satin smooth, noticeably devoid of body hair. The veins in her hands and neck, faintly visible beneath the transparency of her skin were well-defined for a woman's. Runner's veins.

After the past few hours, he was rapidly coming to the conclusion that she was exactly who and what she said she was. He didn't know whether to be dismayed, appalled, or impressed to death that a woman had managed to breach the testosterone fortress of Special Ops.

"You hungry?" he blurted.

She blinked, called back from wherever her thoughts had taken her. "Umm, yes. I guess so."

"Let's go topside. I know a little place on the beach… under the palm trees, drippy candles…the best seafood you ever tasted."

Was that alarm flickering through her gaze? She was so damn hard to read.

She said quietly, "I didn't know we could go to the surface."

"Most of the staff is assigned two-week periods yearly to go topside and act like tourists visiting the island. A few staff members get to pose as people living here, and they can go topside anytime they want."

"Which are you?"

"I'm in the first week of a two-week 'vacation' to the island. I can go up anytime I like. Because you're only here temporarily, you can go up, too."

"Well, then, I guess we're having dinner at your little place on the beach."

Hot damn. And he hadn't even had to let her take him down to get her to agree.

Chapter 3

Jeff hadn't exaggerated the romantic atmosphere of this place. Kat couldn't help but relax and enjoy the ambience of the beachside restaurant. Their table sat under a private tent on the sand. White gauze curtains fluttered around them, and the sounds of silverware on china and clinking glass blended with the rolling crash and retreat of the ocean only a few dozen yards away.

She had to admit he looked…amazing. He wore a charcoal turtleneck, its sleeves pushed up to reveal muscular, tanned forearms. He didn't appear remotely dangerous, even though she knew him to be so. He was elegant. Urbane. Some chameleon.

Of course, he was probably thinking the same thing about her. The Medusas included girly clothes and makeup in their standard operating equipment. Sometimes their best disguise during a mission was to look as feminine and harmless as possible. Hey—sex worked. Get a target thinking about maneuvering you into the sack, and a pistol in your purse or a microphone down your bra was the last thing on his mind.

Tonight she wore a plum silk dress with a high hem and a low neck. Spaghetti straps held up the whisper-soft fabric.

"This spot is beautiful." She sighed appreciatively.

Jeff smiled. "I'm glad you approve. I thought it would be a good place for a beginning between us." He picked up his wineglass. "A toast."

Was he still hung up on that Cupid's Bolt thing? Alarmed, she picked up her crystal stem.

"Here's to a long and fruitful relationship between us," he murmured.

Somehow, she didn't think he was talking about catching the Ghost. She took a sip of the crisp Chardonnay he'd ordered for them and, setting down her glass, said, "Tell me about the stolen art."

"It's an interesting assortment. All the pieces are by masters. Various schools of art, though. A Holbein, a Turner, a Cézanne, a Brecht."

"How valuable?"

He shrugged. "It's hard to place a price tag on these high-end pieces unless you actually take them to auction and see what the collectors are willing to pay. But we're talking two to ten million apiece."

"Why haven't these thefts been all over the news?"

"Shockingly enough, these aren't particularly large thefts. Pieces worth a hundred million or more have been stolen. Those make the network news shows."

"I can't imagine any painting being worth that much," she confessed.

"It's all about covetousness. Having something famous and beautiful all to yourself. You get to look at it and nobody else." He reached out to where her left hand lay on the white linen tablecloth and twined his fingertips with hers. His voice went low and husky. "It's a lot like possessing a beautiful woman.

Except a painting transcends time. People the world over, for decades or centuries, have coveted that piece, and now it's yours."

She replied wryly, "Plus, there's the added advantage that a painting won't get PMS and act bitchy or divorce you and take all your money."

He chuckled and released her hand. "There is that."

Odd. She was faintly disappointed that he'd let go. The feel of his fingers had been nice. "Personally, I'm not crazy about the notion of being possessed by some man."

His smile ran as lazy as a river on a hot summer day. "Then the right man has never possessed you, darlin'. Don't get me wrong. It's not about owning another human being, body or soul. It's about cherishing her. Savoring her, doing anything for her. Making her feel like the most special woman in the world."

Wow. She'd never imagined any man might actually want to treat a woman like that, let alone imagined finding one for herself. Uncomfortable, she retorted lightly, "I dunno. Sounds almost creepy."

He gave her a reproachful look. "There's no need to be evasive with me. If the idea of being loved that deeply scares you, you can tell me. I'll still love you even if you have a human weakness or two under your superhero skin."

She had to catch her jaw to keep it from sagging. First, she was stunned that he'd read her that well. Nobody ever saw past the impassive mask she'd been trained from earliest childhood to show the world. Second, he'd pegged her as superhero material? Granted, she'd tossed him around and employed an old ninja climbing trick, but he'd put his finger on her most closely guarded secret within a few hours of meeting her. She couldn't count the number of times Hidoshi had told her through the years never, ever, to let anyone know what she was truly capable of. He'd warned over and over, "If you show them your skill, they will insist upon testing it."

He was so right. She'd gotten distracted by Jeff's sex appeal in the gym and let down her guard for an instant. A single, simple takedown of the man, and already he'd tested her reflexes twice more—once with a gun. She'd bet the men who'd seen her drop Jeff were just waiting for their chance to have a go at her, too.

As usual, Hidoshi's advice was spot on. Too bad he'd never given her any advice on how to react to a gorgeous lunatic who was convinced she was destined to be his.

The rhythmic crash of the ocean gradually soothed her inner turmoil. As she neared the end of her scallops in cream sauce, she asked, "What do the stolen paintings have in common?"

"None of them are particularly famous, but they're all excellently executed. Perhaps most notable is the fact that all of the pieces have been held by private collectors for most or all their existences."

Kat frowned. "And that's significant why?"

"Museums publish extensive catalogs and prints, and publicly display paintings. Which is to say, museum pieces are vastly more identifiable than privately held pieces."

"Ergo, the privately held piece can be stolen and hung on a new owner's wall with less chance of being recognized as a stolen work."

"Exactly. If a shady collector wanted to flaunt his trophies, he'd need to acquire little-known pieces."

"Is the thief stealing on behalf of a specific collector, or is he stealing pieces he can fence more easily because they're less well-known?"

Jeff smiled broadly. "Well done. That is, indeed, the sixty-four-thousand-dollar question. For a newcomer to the art world, you've put your finger on the heart of the matter astoundingly quickly."

"And you're not a newcomer to it?" she asked in surprise.

"My family has owned an art gallery in New Orleans for over a hundred years."

"Did you work in the business to have learned so much about the art world?"

He winced. "Not entirely. I—" He paused, embarrassed. "—majored in art history in college."

She stared. "How in the world did you end up—" Aware of other ears nearby, she finished circumspectly, "—in our line of work?"

"Easy. Art history majors don't get the hot chicks."

She laughed, startled. "You got into the biz to pick up women? And how's that working out for you?"

His gaze took on a heat that stole her breath away. "So far so good, if I had to make an initial assessment."

"Oh, really?" she asked lightly, butterflies flitting in her stomach. "What makes you think that?"

He tipped the wineglass in his hand slightly in her direction. "The lady's wearing a sexy dress for me. I'd say that's an excellent start."

She shrugged. "It's just what happened to be in my gear bag."

"You haul around sexy little numbers like that in your work gear?" he blurted.

She nodded casually, studying the remnants of her meal. No sense telling him she had several other dresses to choose from and this one *had* been the sexiest of the bunch. His ego was already big enough. She glanced up to find him staring at her in open consternation.

"What?" she demanded.

"What exactly do you ladies *do* in your line of work?"

"The same thing you do. Why?"

"Is that all you do?"

She laid her fork down very gently. "I don't like what you're implying."

"Neither do I," he replied grimly.

She leaned forward and spoke with quietly intensity. "I'll say this once and once only. The Medusas have never been asked to nor have they done anything remotely like what you're thinking in the execution of their job. Understood?"

"Loud and clear, darlin'. And may I say, I'm relieved to hear it. I'd hate to have to ask you to choose between me and your work."

"Excuse me?"

"Well, once we're officially together, I'm not going to be a fan of sharing you with anyone else, particularly some hostile target you've been ordered to romance."

"Jeff. We are not together. Not that I'd personally be comfortable romancing a hostile anyway, but that would be my decision to make—not yours. My job. My career. My decision."

He looked pained. "I never thought I'd end up with a career woman, especially a military one. I wasn't planning on facing these sorts of issues."

"Gee. I'm sorry to have fouled up your grand plan for a nineteenth-century marriage—or did you have something more fourteenth century in mind?"

He grinned. "I have to say, now that I've found you, I'm surprisingly okay with you having a career. Even the one you have."

She rolled her eyes. "Thanks so much for giving me permission to do my job."

His grin widened unrepentantly.

Now that he'd *found* her? He said that like he'd been *looking* for her. Those pesky butterflies were knocking around her stomach again. "For what it's worth, most of the men who've gotten involved with my teammates seem to have struggled initially to accept the danger we place ourselves in."

He frowned. "What sorts of ops do you run?"

Thankfully, the wind had picked up, pushing the waves more noisily onto the beach. With one eye trained on the nearest tents, she replied, "Exactly the same kind you do. Only exception: The missions are profiled to include less heavy lifting and fewer long-distance ingresses and egresses. We're the first to admit that we can't begin to match the strength and stamina of a male team. Our job is to work around that limitation."

He blinked, looking startled at the admission.

"For example, my sniper rig is modified to weigh less than a standard model. I sacrifice some range on my shots, but it's a trade-off. Pass out of exhaustion trying to hump in the weapon to a target, or work my way in for a closer shot and actually make the kill."

"So you're a short-range specialist, then?"

She nodded. "I don't do half bad with a long-range rig. But if I'm hauling my own gear to the kill zone, I usually go short. If I were as big and strong as some of my teammates, I might consider doing more long-range work, though."

"It's daunting to consider women stronger than you. I felt you take me down this afternoon. You're no wimp, honey."

"Nah, I'm the little, quick one on the team. Python and Sidewinder are a lot stronger than I am."

"How many of you are there?"

"Six, plus one prospect in training."

"Any plans to expand the team?"

"You'd have to take that up with General Wittenauer or the president. We'd like to expand the program, though. We've been talking about how to recruit and train more women and the sorts of skills sets we'd look for."

"Like what?"

She smiled. "Well, a big, strong sniper for one. More linguists with a broader range of languages. And—" she broke off. Jeff probably wasn't ready to hear the next idea they'd been tossing around.

"And what?" he prompted.

"Nothing."

His gaze narrowed. "And a few high-priced call girls with a penchant for guns, perchance?"

She jolted. How had he picked that thought out of her brain? She schooled her face to perfect stillness. "An interesting idea. What do you think of it?"

He frowned. "My knee-jerk reaction is to hate the idea of asking women, regardless of previous experience, to use their bodies to do my job."

"And your reaction after you give it some thought?"

He shrugged. "I can see the usefulness of a…skill set…like that. It could certainly open some avenues of intelligence collection that the Special Forces have not traditionally had access to."

"But it would be controversial."

He snorted. "As if the idea of women running around in the Special Forces killing people and blowing stuff up isn't?"

"Well, there is that."

They traded smiles.

He murmured, "I gotta confess, I'm having a little trouble wrapping my brain around the whole idea of women operatives. Had I not seen you do what you did today, I'd be highly skeptical."

"And now you're only moderately skeptical?"

"My shoulder still aches from where you twisted it, my thumb is sore from when you dropped me the second time, and my ego's definitely bruised. When pain's involved, I'm a quick learner."

Hidoshi used to say she would never become a great warrior because she spent all her time trying to avoid getting hit and not attacking. But she'd learned. She could take pain with the best of them now.

She commented. "Lots of male operators get cranky when they first find out about us. They forget we're all playing for the same team. That we uphold and defend the same Constitution and fight for the same values." She looked him squarely in the eye. "You're not going to make that mistake, are you?"

He sighed. "Honestly, I had about as Neanderthal a

reaction to the idea of female operators as the next guy." He looked up at her and grinned. "But then you planted me on my butt. Twice. I guess I'd have to say I'm convinced."

"I didn't really hurt you, did I? I was trying not to."

He grinned ruefully. "I'd hate to see you go at it when you really mean someone harm. Nah, I'm not hurt. Nothing that won't recover. Except maybe my ego. Sometime I want to go one-on-one with you on a mat…when I'm prepared for you to jump me."

She grinned impishly. "It won't help. I'll still win."

He laughed. "Oh, really? Care to place a small wager on that?"

Finally. A natural response to her that he might give to one of his male counterparts. She smiled. "Anytime, any place, big guy. Name your bet."

Chapter 4

When the check came, Kat reached for her purse.

"Don't even think about it," Jeff growled. "My mother would tan my hide if she caught me inviting a woman out and then not paying for the date."

Kat started. This hadn't been a date—had it? Sure, there'd been romantic candlelight and the ocean and the sexy guy, of course. But a date? She didn't do dates. She had no time for them.

Wary, she watched as he stood up and came around behind her chair to hold it for her. His fingertips trailed lightly along her bare shoulder, sending shivers shooting through her. Oh, God. He'd given her goose bumps. She silently prayed he wouldn't notice her reaction to his touch.

"Can I tempt you into a walk along the beach?"

She hesitated to accept the offer. Whatever was happening between them was moving far too fast, slipping out of her control. Caution and control—those had been her mantras her whole life, and they'd never let her down so far.

Jeff coaxed, "I'm pretty sure it's a felony to visit a tropical paradise and not walk on the beach by moonlight."

Caution, indeed. This guy was a runaway freight train! "Jeff—" she started.

He effectively cut off her protest by pulling her seat back and cupping her elbow lightly. Caution and control fluttered away on a warm breeze that smelled of salt air and mystery. One touch from this guy and so much for a lifetime of training. She mentally shook her head in disgust at herself since Hidoshi wasn't there to do it for her.

"Why so quiet all of a sudden?" Jeff asked as they headed toward the water.

She glanced over at him, surprised. "I'm always quiet."

"You don't say much, but I can hear you thinking most of the time."

Startled, she stopped in the act of bending down to kick off her high-heeled sandals. "How?"

"I suppose I'm reading body language. Your eyes are always moving, you're always assessing everything and everyone around you."

"Like you're not? All special operators do that as a matter of habit."

He shrugged. "It's more than a habit with you. It's like you're always waiting for the next attack. You don't always have to be on duty, you know."

She stopped. Turned to face him. The moonlight sculpted his features in pale relief. The man had definitely hit the jackpot in the genetic lottery of looks. "It's not about being on duty or off. This is who I am."

If it was possible for a marble statue to convey skepticism, he did so then, staring down at her for a long time in silence. Finally, he said, "You mean to tell me you have no feelings? No desires? No personal life? Just the job?"

Frustration roiled through her. Of course she had those things. But they were private. To be kept to oneself. Never on display for others to see. "I am not, at heart, American. I am Asian. Old school."

"What does that mean?"

"I was taught not to wear my emotions on my sleeve as you Americans do. I was taught to be…" She didn't know what word to use next. *Refined?* That would insult him by implying that Americans were coarse. *Restrained?* That sounded like she hog-tied her feelings and totally denied them. *Repressed?* Probably accurate, but not exactly something she liked owning up to.

"Kiss me," he ordered abruptly.

Rattled to her core, she sputtered, "I beg your pardon?"

"You heard me. I'm not convinced you actually have any emotions at all. Prove it."

"By kissing you?"

"By kissing me." He braced his feet in the sand, his expression implacable as he stared down at her.

"This is ridiculous. I'm not letting you double-dare me into kissing you like a couple of kids in the schoolyard."

"Ahh. So you're a coward, too," he commented blandly. "I wouldn't have guessed it. I pegged you for more courage than that."

Courage? He dared to question her courage? "Is this the part where I fling myself at you and kiss your lights out to prove how brave and emotional I am?" she retorted scornfully.

"It would help. I'm beginning to have serious doubts over whether or not a heart beats inside your chest or if there's only a robot ticking in there. Which is it?"

Hurt streaked through her. After all his talk of Cupid's Bolt and destiny, how could he say something like that? She whispered, mostly to herself, "Sometimes I ask myself the same question."

He stepped forward so quickly she had no time to evade him. Or maybe something deep inside her didn't want to evade him. Either way, his arms came around her gently, wrapping her in the warmth and shelter of his body. "Ahh, baby, I've looked into your soul. You're all woman in there. You just have to learn to let her out."

Easier said than done. A lifetime of teaching said to do otherwise.

Jeff murmured, "It's not hard. Watch. Like this."

And before she knew what was happening, he'd put his finger under her chin and lifted her mouth to meet his. Shock ripped through her, followed by a melting warmth that all but buckled her legs out from under her. It was an innocent enough kiss, just his lips, warm and firm and gentle on hers. No demands, no invasions, no assertion of macho dominance. And it was all the more seductive for the lack of aggression.

His hair was silky beneath her fingers—how in bloody hell did her hands get around his neck and into his hair? As quickly as the question exploded in her brain, the answer followed, a soft sigh of surrender deep in her soul. Who cared how they got there? The fact was her arms were twined around his neck, her breasts pressed intimately against his chest, his belt buckle jabbing her belly, his muscular thigh rubbing the junction of her thighs as his right arm drew her up more tightly against him.

Oh, my. He felt so…right.

His left hand slid under the weight of her hair at her neck, cupping her head as he sipped at her, kissing and nibbling until a foreign irritation built low in her gut, a driving need for more—more of his touch, more of his mouth and hands upon her, more skin on skin, more *everything.*

She raised up on tiptoe, her mouth opening beneath his, her kisses abruptly—and wholly independent of her will—eager and demanding. Something wild within her wanted more than a hint of this unleashed man. She wanted his passion, his body; heck, his soul.

Jeff broke off the kiss, thankfully panting as hard as she

was. It was with extreme reluctance that she let him go. Only the threat of seeming obsessive and clingy unwound her arms from around his neck. But damn if her palms didn't land on his chest, measuring the bulge of his pectorals. A whole lot of push-ups had gone into those.

"See, Kat? There's a passionate woman in there, waiting to get out." He spoke lightly, but she guessed at the effort that carefree tone took.

His arms fell away and she stumbled back in the deep sand, appalled. She'd just kissed her boss. With tongue. While squirming against him like a cat in heat.

She swore long and hard at herself in every language she knew.

They stood there an embarrassingly long time, both catching their breath and staring at one another in varying degrees of shock. He looked as shaken by what had just happened as she was. Her thoughts spun frantically. Was that a good sign or a bad sign? Had she been a terrible kisser? Was he having second thoughts about his Cupid's Bolt? What if—

She broke off her panicked train of thought sharply. These sorts of thoughts were exactly why she'd sworn off relationships entirely by the time she'd graduated from college. She just didn't need the insecurity and uncertainty of it all.

"I—"

"You—"

They spoke simultaneously, and she was quickest to murmur, "You first."

He huffed in what sounded like frustration. "I ought to apologize, but the only thing I can think of is to ask you to do that again with me. That was…amazing."

The tone in his voice on that last word was almost worshipful. Abject relief turned her innards to jelly. "Really?"

He opened his mouth to answer and she waved a sharp hand to cut him off. "Strike that. I'm not sixteen and don't need the boy to tell the girl he liked kissing her. If you liked it, you'll do it again sometime. If not, I'll live."

He swept her up in his arms before the words had hardly escaped her lips. His mouth swooped down on hers this time with all the aggression—and finesse—she'd expect of a hunky Special Forces soldier who'd had his pick of women for most of his adult life. His body, his mouth, his hands, his *essence,* surrounded her, drew her in to him until she wasn't sure where she ended and he began. It was much more than a kiss. It was a blending of souls. She was staggered by the sensations, both physical and emotional, that he evoked in her so effortlessly.

When he finally lifted his head to smile down at her, she could only stare up at him in shock.

He remarked matter-of-factly, "All right then. I believe we've established that I like kissing you and plan to do it again. Thoroughly and often."

Her toes curled into the cold sand, squishing it up between her toes pleasurably. Thoroughly and often, huh? Her pulse leaped at the thought.

He added ruefully, "I promised you a walk on the beach, didn't I? And I never break a promise." He gestured at the silver strip of sand stretching away from them. "Which do you want? The ocean side or shore side?"

"Which side would your mother tell you to take?"

He grinned. "She'd tell me to walk on the ocean side where the water's deepest and coldest and let you dribble your tender little toes in the foam."

"Well, let's not disappoint your mother," she replied lightly.

He laughed warmly. "Honey, when you give her grand-kids, she'll think you walk on water."

Kids? Them? The mere thought knocked her completely off balance. Jeff steered her along the water's edge, mindful of her tender little toes. Which was ridiculous, of course.

The two of them regularly swam in water much colder than this as part of their training. They both had experienced depths of hypothermia most people never imagined, let alone suffered through. With her small body mass and low body fat, cold water training was particularly miserable for her.

"What are you thinking about?" he murmured. "You're frowning."

She started. She never showed facial expressions if she didn't want to, and at the moment she wasn't going out of her way to exhibit a frown, thank you very much. "I am not frowning," she disagreed.

He stopped and turned to face her. "Are too. I can feel you frowning without even having to look at you."

If she weren't consciously focusing on her expression at the moment, her brows definitely would have slammed together in a big frown. "What? Are you psychic?" she asked lightly.

"It's Cupid's Bolt. We've got a connection, darlin'. I'm tellin' ya. We were meant for one another."

"What's my mood now?"

He grinned. "You're annoyed that I read you like an open book, but it doesn't take being psychic to know that. You're also wildly attracted to me and confused as hell over what to do about it."

"That's a pretty good pickup line. I bet you get lots of girls with the whole 'destined for each other by Cupid's arrow' bit."

One second she was walking down a starlit beach, and the next he'd spun her around to stare up into the face of fury. Although dark shadows shrouded his features, she couldn't miss the genuine anger rolling off him.

"I've never spoken of that to any woman, let alone experienced it with one. It's a long and honored tradition in my family, and I would never use it as a cheap pickup line." His gaze narrowed even more. "Trust me. I don't need a line like that to get laid. I get all the girls I want without it."

After that kiss he'd planted on her, she didn't doubt it. But then a second reaction overcame her. She struggled for a moment to identify it, and then froze in shock. She was jealous. She staggered back from him, stunned that the idea of him sleeping around with women he casually picked up bothered her so much. Something was wrong with her. Her emotions were flying all over the place. She was *never* like this! Her hormones must be out of whack. Or maybe she hadn't gotten enough sleep recently.

Formally, she said, "I apologize if I offended you or your family's honor." She made a low bow of apology with her palms pressed together before her.

She straightened, and Jeff was peering at her quizzically.

"What?" she muttered. "That's how I was taught to apologize."

"Why the bow?"

"If you wanted to strike me, I was giving you an opening to do it."

"Why in hell would I want to do that?"

"To save face, of course."

Comprehension lit his face. "You really were raised in traditional Asian fashion, weren't you?"

"You have no idea."

His hand touched her upper arm and then slid down to her hand. He turned, tucking her hand in his elbow and commenced walking. "Tell me about it."

She never talked about it. Not the grueling hours of workouts, not the secret training methods that elevated her skills beyond what most mortals dreamed of, not the traditional code of honor, passed down for centuries from warrior to warrior. Nor did she talk about the slow death of the ancient way of life that had forced Hidoshi to pass his legacy on to an orphan girl he'd picked up out of a gutter.

Jeff murmured, "I'll tell you about my life if you'll tell me about yours."

To her shock, she heard her voice say, "I was born in Seoul, Korea. My grandfather was from Japan. He raised me on a small farm in the country."

Hidoshi hadn't been her blood relative as far as she knew, but he'd adopted her in an ancient, if not legally recognized, ceremony. More to the point, he'd pulled her off the streets where she'd been wandering as a toddler and had likely saved her life. And then there was everything else. Her education, her martial arts training, the affection and respect he quietly gave her. Somehow, calling him her grandfather wasn't nearly description enough of what he'd meant to her.

"You love him a great deal, don't you?" Jeff murmured.

How *did* he do that? If she didn't know better, she'd say the guy was, indeed, psychic, the way he picked her thoughts out of thin air. "He meant everything to me."

"Past tense. He passed away?"

She nodded.

"When?"

Under normal circumstances, she'd politely change the subject about now, or if someone waxed persistent, she'd tell them outright it was none of their business. But for some reason, she found herself completely lacking in her usual reluctance to talk to Jeff about Hidoshi.

"He died when I was seventeen."

"How did you end up in the States?"

To her knowledge, she'd never answered that question to a single living soul. Only a few anonymous clerks in the American consulate in Seoul knew once and had hopefully forgotten long ago. Jeff stopped walking and turned to face her as if he knew this was something very private and personal to her. He could really stop doing that.

She ventured to look up at him and was startled at the depth of compassion glowing in his gaze. It wrapped around her, offering comfort and quiet understanding. In her own sudden flash of insight, she realized he'd lost someone very

close to him, as well. He knew the pain, the loss and bewil-
derment of her entire world evaporating in an instant. And
maybe that was why she answered his question.

"When I was going through his personal effects, I found
something."

Jeff waited patiently, merely patting her hand a little in
encouragement.

"My birth certificate. I'd never seen it before. I didn't
know—" She hadn't even known her mother's name until
then. It had never occurred to her that Hidoshi might have
tracked the woman down in the opium dens of Seoul's slums
and found a nameless orphan's identity for her. His quiet, un-
swerving love, even in death, had moved her to her first and
only tears after he'd died.

Kat glanced up and realized she'd just been standing there,
remembering, and Jeff was still patting her hand.

She continued, startled by the catch in her voice. "I didn't
know my father was American. I took my birth certificate and
went to the American consulate in Seoul. They researched it
and found out he was a serviceman stationed in Korea at the
time I was born and was known to keep a Korean mistress.
They decided my birth certificate was legitimate and issued
me a U.S. passport. All of a sudden, I was an American
citizen."

"Have you ever met him?"

"I doubt he knows I exist." A spurt of shame took her by
surprise. She'd thought she'd gotten over that long ago. She
shrugged. "But it's okay. I had everything I needed growing up.
I had no need to drop into some foreigner's life and ruin it."

"You're a remarkable woman. Any man would be proud
to call you his daughter."

Suspicious heat filled her eyes. She said lightly, "I have to
give your mother credit. She certainly taught you good
manners."

He grabbed her roughly by the shoulders. "I didn't say that

to be polite, dammit. I mean it. You're smart and beautiful and athletic as hell. You've got it all."

That's what they all said. Hearing the same old line from Jeff disappointed her. She sighed, then replied emotionlessly. "You're doing what everyone does—judging me purely based on what you can see. You don't know me at all."

"Ahh, but that's where you're wrong. We're alike, you and I. We're soldiers. We live by a code of honor most other people scoff at, but we don't care. We can and do kill without regret. It's part of keeping our country safe, so we do it. We take our work seriously and have both made sacrifices, particularly in our personal lives, to do this job we love."

She blinked up at him as he fell silent. She supposed they did know a lot about each other after all, just by the nature of the profession they shared. It took a certain type of person to do what they did.

"Sorry," he muttered. "I don't usually climb on that soapbox. And besides, you know that chorus already." He turned and they continued down the beach in silence.

They'd walked for maybe another ten minutes when Kat noticed lights nestled in the midst of a verdant forest carpeting the mountain that rose steeply on their right. "What's that up there?"

"The Gray estate."

"It looks white to me."

Jeff chuckled. "The mansion is white. But the owners are Carson and Lucy Gray. They own about half of this island."

"Seriously?"

"Yeah. He comes from a shipping family. Owns a big fleet of container ships. He donated the caves to us, in fact. His wife is American. A geologist of some kind. Supervised the construction of the H.O.T. Watch facilities. They have three or four kids now. Nice family. I see them on the beach sometimes."

"How long has the H.O.T. Watch complex been operating?" Kat asked curiously.

"Construction started about five years ago. It's been up and running for about a year."

She nodded. "That would explain why I haven't heard of it before now."

He grinned over at her. "You have your secret Medusa Project, and I have mine."

She smiled back. "Touché."

Without warning, her purse erupted into sound, her cell phone emitting the custom ring that indicated the office was calling. Simultaneously, Jeff reached for his buzzing cell phone.

She flipped open her phone. "Go ahead." No need to identify herself. Anyone who had this number knew who she was.

"Jennifer Blackfoot here. Sorry to interrupt your evening, but we need you and Maverick back here. There's been another robbery."

Chapter 5

J eff thought fast. They needed to get back to the Bat Cave right away. It would take them a good hour to hike from here to a road, get a taxi to the south beach, and board the minisub for the long ride back to the H.O.T. Watch complex. Or they could use the emergency entrance, which was quite a bit closer.

He looked over at Kat's filmy silk dress and asked regretfully, "Is there any chance you can run in that outfit?"

She glanced down in surprise. "Sure. I could do a marathon in this if I had to. Although I'd tear my feet up. I haven't conditioned them for long distances barefoot."

"How 'bout a couple miles on a sandy beach?"

She shrugged. "No problem."

"Let's go, then." He took off running and Kat followed suit. "You set the pace," he told her.

"How big a crisis is this?" she asked, breathing deeply but easily.

"Don't kill yourself, but we need to get there with dispatch."

"Six-minute mile okay, or do you need faster? I can do one four-thirty mile in a pinch. Although on sand…maybe five minutes would be my best time."

He stared in shock.

She loped along beside him as easily and lightly as a gazelle. "I run marathons in my spare time."

He just shook his head. "You're one of a kind."

"Actually not. One of the women on our team is a triathlete. Now *she's* tough to keep up with."

Jeez. They were all superhuman. Scary.

They settled into a hard but steady run down the beach. He tried not to notice how her silk dress fluttered back against her body, outlining it in glorious, flowing detail. She was as graceful in motion as she looked standing still. He immensely enjoyed the pounding surf, the cool night air rushing in and out of his lungs, the wet sand giving gently beneath his feet and the unison he and Kat fell into, side by side, step for step with one another.

After a good two miles at the killer pace, Kat glanced over at him. "How much farther?" she asked.

"Why? You winded?"

She chuckled. "Not at all. Just curious. Actually, I'm just getting warmed up."

He was more than "just warming up," but he could certainly hold this pace for a good long while. "We're almost there. Emergency entrance to the H.O.T. Watch. Highly classified. I'll have to kill you if you tell anyone about it."

She nodded, smiling, and kept running. At least she had the grace to be working hard enough beside him to avoid chatty conversation. But damn, she was in good shape. He'd never met another female who could keep up with him in a full-out run like this.

They rounded a point, and Pirate's Cove arced away before them. The low, ramshackle shape of Pirate Pete's Delivery Service came into view. The courier business was a cover for the H.O.T. Watch's more visible operations on the island, like airplanes and helicopters coming and going and deliveries and departures of large, unmarked crates.

"Over there." He directed her to Pirate Pete's and they stopped under the porch's shadowed overhang. As he dug keys out of his pocket, he commented, "This is the part where you breathe hard after that run and make me feel macho."

"Oh. Sorry." She commenced panting loudly.

He inserted a specially coded magnetic key in the lock and glanced up at her, grinning. "Take it easy on that heavy breathing or the guys on the other end of the surveillance cameras are gonna wonder what we're up to out here."

She glanced around sharply. "I didn't see any cameras—"

"They wouldn't be hidden if you could see them. But trust me. They're here."

The sound of voices erupted behind them and he spun to face this new threat. A group of a half-dozen tourists had staggered onto the beach. The three young couples looked drunk off their asses. Their raucous laughter drowned out the ocean behind them.

"Hey!" one of them called out. "There's some locals. Watch how frien'ly they arrre…" he slurred, weaving purposefully in their direction.

Jeff cursed under his breath. The last thing they needed was to get tangled up with a bunch of drunk kids. He needed an instant distraction. Something that would drive off the intruders—or give him an excuse to drive them off.

He turned to Kat and swept her up in his arms. She went tense, prepared to do him bodily harm.

"Roll with me on this and don't kill me," he muttered. And then he leaned down to plaster his mouth against hers.

She gasped as their lips touched…but then, so did he.

If he'd thought Cupid's Bolt had slammed into him like a brick before, this time it bowled him over like a rushing freight train. She was exactly *right* for him. Perfect. A sense of destiny washed over him. This was the woman he was meant for. He sucked in another surprised breath, and then inhaled her. She tasted like berries, tart and fresh and sweet all at once, and suddenly he was starving.

Her body hummed, as tense as a bow against his, and then all at once she gave way, melting into him, pressing into him as if a wave of need shoved her against him whether she willed it or no. Her hands clutched his shoulders for balance, and his arms tightened around her convulsively.

She sucked hard at his lower lip, pulling him down to her, seeking his tongue and finding it with hers. Her hands crept up to the back of his head while his crept down to her buttocks. They both used their not inconsiderable strength to draw closer to one another. *Good* didn't even begin to describe how she felt against him. Delicious, succulent, opulent images raced through his brain, and none were adequate to describe her or the cravings she evoked in him.

He backed her up against the wall and she wriggled in his arms, straining toward him as hard as he strained toward her, wild in her need. He drank in her desire, as greedy for her as she was for him. Avidly, he absorbed her essence, learning the delicate but iron-strong feel of her, savoring the faint floral scent that seemed to hang around her, touching her satin hair and the softer satin of her skin.

"Hoo, baby! Look'ee at 'em goin' at it! You go, guy!"

Jeff lurched as he abruptly remembered the drunks behind them. He tore his mouth away from hers to glare over his shoulder. "Can't you see we're busy? Go find your own dark corner to neck in. This one's occupied."

"Well, daa-amn, I guess so, dude. Youze two's throwin' sparks all the way to Miami. Git out the fire extinguisher, Roscoe!" one of the drunks caterwauled back.

He continued to glare at them steadily, letting overt threat infuse his body language. In his experience, it took strong signals and a few extra seconds for drunks to perceive peril.

He held his pose, a promise of violence glinting dangerously in his gaze.

Finally, sluggishly, the group registered the menace he posed. One of the girls grabbed a guy by the arm. "C'mon," she whined. "I wanna swim in the ocean."

Another girl piped up. "I wanna skinny-dip. First guy there gets to take off my bra."

With a whoop, the young men took off running, tripping and stumbling in the sand, the girls trailing behind. Their laughter faded into the roar of the waves. Jeff watched until they disappeared around the point, and then he turned back to Kat.

"Now, where were we?" he murmured.

"What's happening?" Kat whispered. "What is this between us?"

"This, my dear, is grandmama's bolt. Hits ya kinda hard, doesn't it?"

"Like lightning," she grumbled.

He laughed quietly. "Nothing to do for it but to sit back and enjoy the ride." He pushed a lock of sable hair out of her eyes. "Who'd have guessed you'd be the one? Never in a million years did I expect you."

She tensed in his arms. "What's wrong with me?"

"Not a blessed thing. You're perfect." He leaned down to show her how perfect she was, this time kissing her gently, letting his lips slide across hers, letting their tongues play lightly, sipping sweetly at each other. The pounding lust of a minute ago was less hurried now, still driving spikes of need deep into his gut, but with quiet assurance that time to explore this thing between them was near at hand.

"I've never..." She hesitated.

He prompted, murmuring against her lips, "Never what?"

"Never...felt like this before. What are you doing to me?"

"This is commonly referred to as kissing. Or necking, or canoodling, if you want to be old-fashioned. It's when a boy and a girl mash mouths together and swap spit while fantasizing about doing much messier and more intimate things with each other."

She laughed, a breathy wisp of humor that shot straight to his groin. "Thanks. I got that part. How is it that of all the guys I've ever kissed, you make me feel like this? I mean, like you said, a kiss is just mashing mouths and trading saliva."

He jerked back far enough to look down at her. "How many guys are we talking about, here?"

She blinked up at him, startled. A slow smile spread across her face. "Enough to know you're the best kisser I've ever gone out with."

"Honey, I'm the last kisser you're ever going out with."

Skepticism shone in her gaze, but he ignored it. "So, you like kissing me? I like kissing you, too. You taste like blueberries."

"Blueberries?"

He nodded, dropping light kisses across her neck to her cheek and back to her mouth. "You never know when you bite into a blueberry if it's going to be sweet or sour, but it tastes uniquely like blueberry either way. When I touch you, I don't know if you're going to toss me on my butt or kiss me till my hair catches fire, but I know I'm gonna love it either way."

That garnered several owl blinks out of her. "You like me tossing you?"

"Actually, it hurts. A lot. But I love the fact that the woman I'm going to marry can plant me on my butt now and then. Not that you'll ever need to. I'm going to spoil you so bad you'll never need to lift a finger."

"M-marry?"

As he closed the inches between them for another lingering kiss, he murmured, "Mmm-hmm. It's fate, darlin'. Cupid's Bolt always strikes true…."

And then all thought of bolts went right out of his head as Kat kissed him back. They might just have enjoyed a gourmet meal, but darned if she didn't make him hungrier than a bear in the spring. He wanted more of her. A lot more.

Both of them were breathing hard when Kat slid right, holding his hands, to draw him away from the porch.

"Ow!"

His senses went on to instant alert. Who or what had hurt her? "What's wrong?" he replied quickly.

"I banged into something sharp…" She turned in his embrace to examine the wall. "It's this knob."

Knob—oh, Christ. The H.O.T. Watch intercom. The summons to the bunker. They'd been standing out here trading lungs, and the folks downstairs were waiting for them.

A horrifying thought popped into his head. Had they been pressing on the intercom button all this time? Transmitting their steamy kiss to an audience below? He closed his eyes in despair. "Did you just bang into the button now, or have you been leaning on it?" he asked reluctantly.

"I just hit it."

Thank God. He didn't need Kat taking endless ribbing from his guys. They wouldn't bug him too much because he'd take them out on the practice floor and break them in half. Although, now that he thought about it, Kat might do the very same thing to them.

"Ready to face the lions in their den?" he sighed.

A pause. "Oh, yeah—work."

He swung open the concealed panel beside the front door to reveal a palm telemetry reader. He laid his hand on the pliable gel surface, which squished up between his fingers slightly. A click in the door lock indicated he'd been recognized. He turned the knob and stepped inside.

"Thanks," he commented to the dark interior of the store, or more precisely, to whatever duty controller downstairs at the other end of the security cameras had let them in. "This way," he said, leading Kat quickly toward the storeroom behind the counter.

A loud voice erupted without warning from the large birdcage in the corner. "*Baawk!* Pirate Pete is a dirty old bird. Repeats everything that he's heard. Especially the bits about asses and tits—"

Jeff called out sharply, "Shut up, Pete!" To Kat, he muttered, "Sorry. That's Pirate Pete. He's a parrot. With a filthy mouth, I might add."

"Shut up, Pete!" the bird squawked.

Kat giggled.

The sound was incongruous coming from her. Particularly since at the moment, her knees were deeply bent, her hands held shoulder high before her, and everything about her announced her readiness to kill something right here, right now. Apparently, when Pete had opened his big beak, she'd used those lightning-fast reflexes of hers to drop into a defensive stance.

She straightened to her full height, relaxing from the battle alert Pete's outburst had thrown her into. Jeff commented, "In case I haven't mentioned it yet, your reflexes are freaking unbelievable."

She shrugged as he opened the storeroom door, using a keypad and a retinal scanner this time.

"In here." He led the way into a cluttered storeroom littered with packing boxes, rolls of tape, and garbage bags full of packing peanuts. And dust. Lots of dust.

Using the tiny penlight on his key ring, he found his way over to what looked like a circuit breaker box in the corner. "If you'll close the door…" he instructed over his shoulder.

Throwing him a perplexed look, she did as he asked.

He pushed on one of the circuit breakers, which was actually an elevator switch, and the room lurched. Kat grabbed at the nearest shelf in surprise to steady herself.

He grinned. "The entire room is an elevator. Cool, huh?"

She grinned back. "Very cool."

They rode downward for nearly a minute, the silence between them so thick with the memory of the steamy kisses they'd just shared that he could hardly breathe. *Work, buddy. Focus on work.*

The storeroom/elevator lurched gently to a stop. "You can open the door now," he said.

She did so, and one of the familiar stone tunnels of H.O.T. Watch headquarters stretched away from them. He followed her out of the elevator, unabashedly enjoying the view of her pert little derriere.

She asked curiously, "How do people navigate around here? All the halls and doors look the same."

"They're supposed to. When you get assigned to work down here, the first job you're given is to memorize a map of the place. If any intruder were ever to get in, he'd have a hell of a time finding his way around."

She nodded. "That's what I figured."

Man, she was quick on the uptake. He'd bet she was hell on wheels when it came to gathering intelligence from live targets. She'd talk circles around ordinary mortals. But then, all she probably had to do was flash those big brown eyes of hers and her targets would sing like Pavarotti.

"This way." He headed right.

"Is this really a hollowed-out volcano?" she asked as they strode down the hall.

He matched her businesslike tone. If she had the discipline to set aside for the moment what they'd just done together, he could, too. "Yup, this is an extinct volcano. Problem with most natural caves is too much water. And with all the electronics we needed to put in this facility, we had to find a dry cave system. Volcanic remnants are often dry cave networks."

"Aren't they occasionally very hot, lava-filled places, too?" she asked.

He grinned down at her. Their gazes met and instant sparks leaped between them. Hah. So she hadn't entirely put their kiss from her mind. His ego was unaccountably gratified. Belatedly, he answered, "We've been assured this volcano is extinct. But just in case, we have seismic sensors all over the island to monitor Mount Timbalo."

She threw him a skeptical look, but then he stopped in front of another anonymous door, opening it for her. She brushed past him, and yet again, their gazes snapped to one another. Oh, yeah. She was as aware of him as he was of her. Her mouth twitched for the barest instant into a smile, and then she was back to being all business. He followed her into the Ops Center.

The sheer size of the main control room never failed to daunt him a little. Kat, in front of him, hesitated before striding toward the cluster of people at a console in the middle of the room. They were staring up at one of the Jumbotrons in the far wall.

He glanced up. Monet's study for his painting, *The Poppies near Argenteuil*, shone down at him. Jeff winced. The Ghost was moving up in the world. That had to be a twenty million dollar painting if it was worth a cent. No doubt the pressure to catch the thief was going to ratchet up commensurately. Sighing, he walked over to his boss.

Navy Commander Brady Hathaway glanced up at him. "You know the painting?"

Jeff nodded. "Where was it?"

"The Valliard estate."

Another one of the fabulous estates of the Golden Mile. The Valliard place was not the largest among them, but was touted as one of the most opulent. "Did the Ghost take any other paintings?"

"Just the one," Hathaway replied. "There are other valuable pieces in the house. Why only this one?"

Jeff shrugged. "He may have a specific buyer for this piece, or he may prefer to travel light."

Kat added, "The thief may also want to limit his risk and only take time to steal a single piece."

Jeff nodded. "Could be." To Hathaway, he said, "When did the theft happen?"

"Sometime in the past twenty-four hours. A caretaker

reported it stolen about an hour ago. Said he walked through the main house yesterday afternoon and everything was intact. But when he went through tonight, the painting was cut out of its frame."

Jeff cursed under his breath. That was an enormous window of opportunity for the thief. He kept hoping for a theft where the Ghost would have to work fast. It would tell them a lot more about the thief's M.O. But to date, all the thefts had been of unoccupied estates. The winter season didn't start for a few more months, bringing the residents of the Golden Mile to its tropical shores. Of course, at the rate he was going, the Ghost would have picked the island clean long before then.

Kat asked him, "What's the common link between all the paintings?"

He'd been over that a thousand times from every conceivable angle. "They've got no common thread except that they're excellent, if little-known, pieces by masters."

"Any chance I can make a phone call to a colleague about this?" Kat asked.

Jennifer Blackfoot glanced over at Hathaway. The two exchanged a nod and Jennifer said, "There's a phone right here. Any help would be appreciated."

Jeff listened with interest to Kat's one-sided conversation.

"Viper, it's Cobra. Sorry to call you so late. Did I wake you up? Morning sickness at night? That sucks. Hey, I have a problem. We're trying to find a link between a half-dozen paintings that have been stolen recently. Can you get a minute or two on the super array to run them and see if there's some obscure link between them? Great. I'll send you an e-mail with the information in the next few minutes. You rock."

Kat hung up the phone and looked up at him. "Do you have a detailed inventory of the paintings?"

"I'll have to add the Monet to it, but that'll only take a minute. Were you talking about the supercomputer array at the Pentagon, by any chance?"

Kat nodded.

"Your friend will have to wait for weeks to get time on that puppy. It's booked up solid."

Kat grinned. "Not for her. Besides the fact that the Medusas can usually get time on the basis of operational necessity, Viper knows a bunch of the computer techs who work on the array. A couple of them owe her favors."

Jeff nodded. Ahh. The ubiquitous favor owed. Special Forces types had a tendency to collect long lists of people who owed them one. When it was your job to save the world and help people out of impossible binds, gratitude frequently followed suit—along with offers to repay the favor.

He sat down at a computer terminal. It was an easy matter to look up an online catalog listing Monet's works and cut and paste information about the newest theft into his existing list of stolen works. He glanced over at Kat. "Where do I send this file?"

She rattled off an e-mail address, and he hit the send button. He highly doubted this Viper person and her supercomputer would have any success, but he was grateful for any help he could get.

"Incoming call for Captain Steiger," Carter Beigneaux announced from the next row of consoles over. "It's General Wittenauer. I'll patch it to your station."

Great. No doubt the Old Man was calling to breathe fire down his shorts to get cracking on catching the Ghost. Sympathetic glances came his way from the people standing nearby. Wittenauer was a great guy until he didn't get exactly what he wanted. And then, watch out.

The phone in front of Jeff buzzed and he picked it up. "Good evening, sir."

"Evening. You hear about the latest theft?"

"Yes, sir. I'm in the Ops Center right now looking at a picture of the stolen piece."

"Any idea who did it or how?"

"I assume it was the Ghost, but that has not been confirmed."

"Time to take your theories operational, Maverick. Now that you've got Cobra to help, I want the two of you to take direct action to stop this guy. I'm catching all kinds of heat over this."

Jeff grimaced. He knew the feeling.

The general continued. "I want you two to go to Barbados. Catch this guy, dammit."

"This is a police matter, sir—"

"You and Cobra are smarter than the average bear. Use your heads. Be creative. Come up with a way to bag this guy that the police haven't thought of. And do it fast."

Gee. No pressure there. Jeff stared at the receiver as the line went dead. He glanced up at Kat. Her face betrayed not a hint of expression, but he knew without question that she was as surprised at he was to get this order to go operational. How he knew that, he had no idea. Maybe a few of grand-mère's psychic genes had come down to him, after all.

He commented to the gang in general, "Looks like our research project just turned into a mission. Who's the lucky dog who gets to control it from this end?"

Jennifer Blackfoot spoke up. "I'll take it. Knowing you, Maverick, you're going to piss off the local authorities and need my special touch to keep your carcass out of hot water—or, in your case, more like boiling oil." She glanced over at Kat. "If he ticks you off, you have my permission to kick his butt."

Kat nodded with an outward serenity he doubted she was actually feeling while everyone else grinned widely. But then Kat startled him by asking Jennifer, "Which one of us is in charge?"

He started. He'd assumed he'd lead the mission since it had been his baby first. But now that she mentioned it, maybe that wasn't such a straightforward assumption. He and Kat were both captains by rank. Both experienced field operators. Both capable of leading a combat team. Hathaway and Jennifer exchanged another one of those wordless looks of colleagues who've worked together for a long time and know how the other one thinks.

Hathaway looked over at Kat. "You okay with Maverick spearheading this thing?"

She shrugged. "Sure. No problem."

Jordan Yokum, one of his guys in the gym earlier, snickered. "If you pick it by who can kick whose keester, the chick ought to be running the show."

Jeff surged to his feet and had Jordy by the throat all in one move. "You wanna talk about her, you do it with respect, buster. She's a hell of fighter, and she can rip your head off in a New York second. If you call her a chick again, I'm gonna order her to do it. She's Captain Kim to you, or you can call her ma'am. Got it?"

The vignette froze in time as everyone went perfectly still around him. Theirs was a notoriously polite community because their capacity to cause violent harm to one another was so great. A confrontation like this was rare and dangerous.

Kat spoke quietly from behind him. "Thanks for the knight in shining armor bit, Jeff. But it's okay. I'll take care of what your guys call me."

He realized in shock that the fury coursing through him was completely out of proportion to the provocation. Why in hell was he already so possessive of her? He'd known her for approximately eight hours. Yeah, they'd kissed, but he'd kissed plenty of women he'd just met and never roared to their defense like this. She was right. He had no business designating himself the official defender of her honor. Especially when she could, indeed, kick her own asses.

He turned Jordy's neck loose and took a step back.

The other man mumbled, "Hey, man. I'm sorry. I didn't mean to piss you off."

Jeff shook his head. "No, I overreacted. My fault."

Hathaway said grimly, "My office, Jeff. Now."

Crap. He was gonna get a serious butt-chewing, and he deserved it, too. Even Jordy threw him a sympathetic look as he turned to follow his boss.

Kat said behind him, "If someone will show me to Captain Steiger's office, I'll pack my gear. I gather General Wittenauer wants the two of us to leave right away for Barbados. Who around here can arrange for our transportation?"

Gratitude flooded through him. Her comment, made plenty loud enough for Hathaway to hear, was a clear statement of support, an unequivocal announcement that she still wanted to work with him, despite his Neanderthal outburst of a moment before. It would go a long way toward making the upcoming conversation with his boss easier. She didn't have to do it. But she had. Publicly.

Son of a gun.

Maybe the lady liked him for more than just his magnificent kissing, after all.

Chapter 6

Kat was surprised when the guy who'd called her a chick in the Ops Center poked his head into Jeff's warehouse/office a little while later.

"Captain Kim? Captain Steiger will meet you at the boat dock in fifteen minutes. I'm supposed to take you down there."

She rose easily out of the cross-legged pose she'd been sitting in, meditating in a futile effort to relax and re-center herself. If she were being brutally honest, she'd been trying to erase the memory of Jeff's kisses and her reaction to them. And frankly…it was not happening.

In less than a day, one man had undone twenty-five years' worth of intensive training and self-discipline instilled by one of the great martial arts masters of his time. She didn't know whether to be intrigued as hell or scared to death of Jeff Steiger. Either way, she was horribly discombobulated and out of balance.

If she couldn't actually be calm, at least she could fake it. She spoke smoothly to the nervous man before her. "You can call me Cobra if you like."

He smiled gratefully, acknowledging the offer of her field handle as the gesture of forgiveness it was. "I didn't mean anything by that comment, you know. Maverick can whup all our butts. And the way you took him down today, I figure you can whup all of ours, too."

No doubt she could. But she wasn't about to comment on it. "All's forgotten," she murmured. She picked up her gear bag and rifle case. "Lead on..." She left the sentence hanging.

He obligingly filled in with his field handle. "Chain. Short for Chainsaw."

She quirked an eyebrow. "Hmm. An evocative handle."

"In BUDS, my trainers accused me of having the subtlety of a chainsaw. The name stuck."

"Well, at least it didn't have anything to do with your massacre weapon of choice."

He grinned. "Can I take one of those bags for you?"

"No, thanks. I've got them. I didn't know this place had a boat dock."

"It's left over from a smuggling operation that ran out of these caves briefly a few years back. It's at the other end of the facility, though. Bit of a hike. Sure you don't want me to get one of those?"

"I've carried these bags to hell and back. I'll be all right."

"Maverick said you're a Special Forces type. Did you do the dreaded eighty-mile march, too?"

She rolled her eyes in recollection of the Special Forces training rite of passage. "Ugh. Did you have to remind me of that?" Normally, she wouldn't be even remotely this talkative with a stranger, but the guy was trying so hard to make up to her that she felt obliged to throw him the bone.

"Yup, that was a bitch—" He broke off abruptly and started to stammer an apology.

She replied gently, "Unlike Maverick, I'm not going to bite your head off for using the B-word in front of me. I've been known to use it myself, and I'm sure I qualify to have it applied to me now and then. Captain Steiger seems to have a rather old-fashioned view of how women should be treated. But we Medusas aren't tense about such things, particularly around our colleagues."

From her, that was quite a speech. But the guy seemed sincerely sorry and also seemed badly in need of a little reassurance that he and she were square.

Chain glanced over at her curiously. "Is there really a whole team of you women operators?"

"Yes."

"I gotta say, I'd like to see you all in action sometime."

"Who knows? Maybe you will. We haven't done much training in this part of the world. We may head down this way someday."

"That'd be cool. As long as I didn't have to spar with you. You moved like lightning in that gym."

She suppressed a smile. She'd actually jumped Jeff pretty casually in the gym. Her move-now-or-die speed was quite a bit faster than that. They walked the rest of the way to the dock in silence. Chainsaw seemed satisfied that peace was restored between them, and indeed, in her mind, it was.

The Medusas had learned to have thick hides when it came to initial skepticism from their male counterparts. They'd also learned long ago to let their actions speak for them and not to rise to verbal baiting. The only thing perplexing to her about the whole "chick" incident was why Jeff had reacted so violently.

They arrived at the dock, and a burst of heat flooded her at the sight of Jeff waiting beside a sleek powerboat. Lord, he was good-looking. Head-turning handsome. Her hands itched with the memory of that muscular chest and washboard waist sliding beneath her palms. Conversing casually with the boat's driver, he oozed confidence. Charisma. Ease with command.

When he saw her coming, he climbed aboard the vessel and reached out to take her bags from her. Their gazes met, and his gleamed hotly with inappropriate thoughts…no doubt the same inappropriate thoughts streaking through her head. She looked away hastily.

She started to climb aboard and wasn't surprised when he held a hand out to help her. Normally, she'd ignore such offers. After all, her balance was superb. But she took Jeff's proffered hand anyway. Of course, it had nothing to do with her ongoing craving to touch him, to feel his energy flowing through her, yin to yang, chi to chi.

His fingers were warm and strong and steady and sent a rush of something feminine fluttering through her. And then an awful thought struck her. He was her *boss* now. First order of business was to quit touching him. Regret stabbed her. And kissing—definitely no more kissing. Darn it.

"Buckle in," Jeff murmured. "This baby can fly."

The driver nodded over his shoulder at both of them and the vessel leaped forward, skimming across the black, glassy surface of the Caribbean, circling around Timbalo Island in mere minutes and pulling up at a wooden pier. She followed Jeff to shore, where a helicopter waited for them. With the ease of long experience with the birds, she stepped under the rotors and passed her bags to Jeff inside the sleek Eurocopter EC 155 with its distinctive built-in tail rotor.

She climbed inside and wasn't surprised when Jeff took the seat directly across from her. The helicopter lifted off and she asked him, "How long to Barbados?"

"An hour and change at top speed."

She nodded. Paused. Nope, she couldn't resist. "Mind if I ask you a question?"

He flashed her those killer dimples of his. "Anything, darlin'. My life is an open book to you."

"Why'd you get so mad at Chainsaw for calling me a chick? Believe me, I've been called a lot worse and I'm still in one piece."

His eyes went a turbulent shade of sapphire. "Commander Hathaway asked me the same thing."

"What'd you tell him?"

"I told him I expect my men to act like gentlemen and didn't appreciate Chain calling you that. I mentioned the need for my guys to accept the reality of female Special Forces operatives, too, I think."

"In other words, you didn't tell him the truth. Did he buy your answer?"

Jeff's dimples flashed. "Not for a second. But he didn't press me on it."

"Why *did* you jump him?"

He gave her a reproachful look. "Do you really have to ask? Even Commander Hathaway knows the answer to that one without having to hear me say it."

An urge to gulp nearly overcame her. While it was flattering in the extreme to have a guy this charming and handsome and sexy laying claim to her like this, she wasn't at all sure how it was going to impact their mission.

"What's wrong?" he murmured.

Her frown deepened. She wasn't even sure she could put it into words. "What have you done to me?"

The corner of his mouth tipped up. "I kissed you. And given how flummoxed you seem, I'd say I made quite an impression on you."

"You don't have to look so satisfied with yourself." She grumbled.

His smile broadened, but he wisely made no reply.

"You don't understand—" she started.

"Then explain it to me. What's got your feathers so ruffled?"

She exhaled hard. "I'm...a warrior." She paused, searching for words.

"So am I. And your point?"

She glanced up, relieved to see he wasn't laughing at her. In fact, he seemed to be concentrating intently on her. Which was perhaps more unnerving. "My life is devoted to a principle. To discipline. To duty. To…honor."

He nodded encouragingly, apparently still waiting for the big reveal.

"That's it," she huffed. "That's the problem. I don't have time for…other pursuits."

"Why ever not? My life is about honor and discipline and duty, but I still have time for a personal life."

"I don't see you with a wife and two kids and a minivan."

He shrugged. "I hadn't met you yet."

"But don't you see? I'm not about having two kids and a minivan!"

He stretched his legs out until his ankles tangled with hers. "That is going to present us with some logistical issues, isn't it? I understand your desire for a career. Hell, I'm not ready to hang up the old rifle yet. I guess we can wait until we're both done with the Special Forces to start a family."

Exasperation shot through her. "Will you quit talking like I've already agreed to marry you? I'm not even sure I want to date you!"

"But you want to kiss me again, don't you?"

An urge to scream bubbled up in her throat. Damn if he wasn't exactly right. She took a deep breath, held it for a count of ten and then released it very slowly. Familiar calm flowed over her, washing away the foreign emotions cluttering her thoughts.

She would face this problem head on. Calmly. Rationally. Honestly. "Yes, I do want to kiss you again. I want to do a lot more than that with you."

He sucked in a sharp breath as she continued. "I also know it is not the right thing to do and it would interfere with the mission. Therefore, I shall set my desires aside and focus on the task at hand."

"Just like that?" He sounded surprised.

"Just like what?"

"You can turn off your feelings like a light switch? No random imaginings of getting naked with me? No speculation on what making love with me would be like? No trouble keeping your gaze from going places it shouldn't? You can just decide to set all that aside, and it's done?"

She blinked, startled. She hadn't really considered if the actual execution of her plan would be hard or not. She'd only gotten as far as it being the right thing to do.

He leaned forward abruptly, startling her. He popped her lap belt and dragged her across the space between them and onto his lap. She should've broken his wrist, but somehow she ended up sprawled across his thighs, his mouth slanting down toward hers, his hands plunging into her hair, and she let him.

Somehow she ended up arching toward him, her body taut with need. Somehow her mouth ended up plastered against his, her hands moving frantically across his chest, her entire being vibrating with uncontrollable need. Somehow the buttons of his shirt opened beneath her fingers, her palms flattened against his hot flesh. A moan escaped her throat and she all but crawled inside him. She turned in his arms until she faced him, straddling his hips with her thighs. How her own shirt fell open, she had no idea. But when his hands closed upon her throbbing breasts, she didn't think twice about pressing more deeply into his hands, about writhing on the hard bulge between her legs, about making a good-faith effort to extract his tonsils with her tongue.

Jeff murmured laughingly, "Honey, my hat's off to you if you can turn this off on command. There's not a chance I can do it."

Whether it was a sigh or a sob that escaped her lips, she

wasn't sure. But she knew she wanted him worse than she'd ever wanted anything in her life. Beneath his clever hands she danced, responding to every touch, every caress, every stroke and pluck upon her aching body. How her pants got unzipped, she had no idea, but she couldn't fail to notice when his fingers invaded her most private space, driving her half out of her mind. Pleasure completely overtook rational thought, spinning her up and out of herself, to a place of heat and light and tingling sensation that took her breath away.

And Jeff was there, all around her, between her thighs, against her breasts, kissing her neck, breathing her in. And it felt…so…good.

Eventually thought stopped altogether, and she flung herself into the drowning glory of the moment.

"Honey, you're killing me," he muttered.

She pulled back to stare at him. "I'm not hurting you, am I?"

He responded with a pained laugh. "I thought you were the one who was supposed to be able to turn off this thing between us. Don't count on me to be all noble and stop it. I'm not that strong."

What was "this thing" between them, anyway? She struggled to form intelligent thought, but the current of her lust was incredibly powerful and sweeping her wildly forward toward oblivion.

"What have you done to me?" she managed to whisper.

"Bluntly put, I believe I've turned you on. And Lord knows, you've done the same to me. Ain't it grand?"

She laughed ruefully and pressed her forehead against his. Grand didn't even scratch the surface of it. "We've got to stop, you know."

"Yeah. I know. Here I go, setting you off my lap, buttoning up our shirts and thinking serious, mission-related thoughts." He didn't move a muscle as he uttered those words, other than to run his fingers through her hair, smoothing strands of it lightly across her breasts.

How had her hair gotten out of its usual French braid?

"Okay, your turn to do something," he muttered.

"Right. I'm climbing off you. Going back to my own seat. Meditating until my mind is clear." Her fingers traced the line of his jaw, the outline of his ears, the shape of his mouth.

"We're formulating our plan of attack for Barbados now," he mumbled. "First order of business…take you to our hotel room and get you naked…"

She nodded soberly but couldn't keep the twinkle out of her eyes. "And then we talk to the police and come up with a brilliant plan to trap the Ghost while lying in bed together watching the sun rise."

He laughed. "I love the way you think."

Gradually, sanity was beginning to return to her. She sighed. "And then the Ghost gets away, we fail at our mission, and we let down General Wittenauer and American citizens who are counting on us."

The laughter in his eyes dimmed. "There is that."

She looked deep into his cobalt-blue eyes. "What are we going to do?"

He sighed. "I suppose we're going to try it your way for a while."

His big hands spanned most of her waist as he gently lifted her off his lap and placed her back in her own seat. Abruptly abashed at her earlier boldness, she fixed her clothes and re-braided her hair. She ventured a gaze over at Jeff, and he was studying her inscrutably. Had he really succeeded at shutting down his lust? What was the world coming to when a fun-loving good ols' boy had more discipline than a highly trained martial arts master?

He murmured, "Working with you is going to be a royal pain in the ass, you know."

"Why?" she blurted.

"Because we've got to set this thing between us aside for now. And I'm going to spend every waking minute wanting to put my hands on you again and hear you make those sounds again and taste you again…"

She gulped. Oh. Yeah, that.

Okay. So deciding not to have any feelings for him and not to react to him hadn't worked out so well. Time for Plan B. They might not be able to control what they thought or felt, but at least they could control what they did. And they both obviously lost all self-discipline once they touched each other. From here on out they were simply going to have to observe a strictly hands-off policy. No kissing, no handholding, no casual brushes against each other. Yup, it was going to suck rocks. But what other choice did they have?

Chapter 7

They pulled up in front of police headquarters in their rental car a little before midnight. She observed while Jeff did the talking. He was very smooth and managed to extract a few details about the latest theft, but the police held their cards close to the chest.

Kat and Jeff wandered toward the exit, and when no one was paying attention, ducked down a side hall that brought them to the evidence locker. Jeff flashed her a Special Forces hand signal to fall back. One eyebrow raised, she did so, fading into the shadows well down the hallway.

And then his tactic became clear. He bellied up to the check-in window and plied his considerable Southern charm on a female evidence officer, who in short order was hanging over the gate and flirting right back at him. Kat had to give him credit. The woman was putty in his hands in a matter of minutes.

Almost as fast as she'd succumbed to him, dammit.

Kat barely registered the additional details he coaxed out of the woman. If that woman leaned much farther forward, she was going to fall out of her uniform. Jeff must be getting an eyeful of the woman's ample cleavage. Only one painting taken last night from the Valliard place.

Oh, and now the chick was fondling her top button, toying with the idea of "accidentally" slipping it free. Hussy. The Monet was, indeed, stolen sometime in the past twenty-four hours.

If that woman licked her lips one more time, Kat was going to lick them for her—with her knuckles. The police strongly suspected the Ghost based on the complete lack of evidence left behind.

Jeff pocketed the slip of paper with the woman's phone number on it and turned to sashay down the hall. Kat fell in behind him, closing on his six like a dutiful wingman.

Not that she felt the least bit dutiful at the moment, however. Equal parts fury and humiliation swirled in her afterburners, making for an explosive mix. Had she fawned all over him like that? Had he flashed her a smile and a suggestive look or two over dinner and then watched her fall into his arms on cue? He was insufferable to behave like that! And she was a fool to have fallen for him like some gullible groupie.

Except that his desire for her had been real. She might not know much about men, but she was dead certain he hadn't been faking in the helicopter. *Desire* being the operative word, however. For all his big talk about her being his soul mate, so far he'd only actually displayed a large dose of healthy male lust for her. And he'd turned on the charm for another woman fast enough.

Hah. And he said he never used sex to help with his work. She might have hassled him about it, but she had no desire to further probe the little green monsters bouncing around in her stomach.

One thing she knew for sure. She was a mess. How Jeff

Steiger had managed to throw her this totally off balance this fast, she had no idea. But she didn't like it. When they got to their hotel, she was having a nice long meditation and getting him thoroughly out of her system—regardless of her failure to do so in the helicopter.

As for the job at hand, there wasn't much to mull over about the theft. There was no sign of forced entry. An excellent security system had inexplicably been circumvented. The caretaker had worked there for thirty-five years and had an airtight alibi for last night, not to mention a sterling reputation on the island. It was the Ghost, through and through.

On their way out of the police station, they ran into the detective in charge of the art theft investigation. The guy seemed none too pleased that they were still hanging around.

Jeff asked the detective, named Elgin D'Abeau, "Would you mind if we went out and had a look at the Valliard place in the morning?"

All guise of friendliness evaporated. "Sorry, mon. Dis is a police mattuh. Stay out of it, and tell your people to stay away, too."

Kat assumed that by "your people," the detective meant the American government. Yikes. Lack of police cooperation would spell big trouble for their op. Time for a quick intervention.

She spoke up smoothly. "As you know, Detective, Mr. Steiger represents certain American interests. I, however, do not." She caught the flash of surprise in Jeff's eyes, and also how quickly he masked it. He was good, all right.

Time for a little flirtation of her own. After all, what was good for the gander was good for goose. She smiled intimately at D'Abeau and let her hand drift up to the detective's shoulder seemingly of its own accord.

"Actually, I work for Lloyd's of London—" her hand drifted lower. Slid off his elbow and fluttered to her throat. "I'd appreciate it if you could keep that under your hat—you understand—the sensitive nature of this case—"

She tucked a lock of errant hair behind her ear, running her fingertip suggestively around her earlobe. She let her voice go breathy and took a small step forward, bringing her subtly but definitely into the guy's personal space. "I wouldn't dream of interfering in any way, of course—"

His nostrils flared, and his pupils expanded sharply as he nodded in agreement.

Time to go for the kill. "My employer is deeply concerned about this string of thefts and Lloyd's would like to offer any assistance we can in the matter. I'll see to it personally." Loaded emphasis on the *deeply* and the *personally,* of course.

The detective swayed forward, a slow grin unfolding on his face. He purred back, "Of course, Ms. Kim. I completely understand."

She'd bet he did. She continued in her huskiest voice, dripping with all the sex she could muster. "Of course, my firm wouldn't want to cause a fuss by advertising my presence here—perhaps even scare certain residents into leaving the island. I must ask that you exercise the utmost discretion regarding mentioning my affiliation—deeply appreciative and all. Our intent is to stay completely clear of your investigation, of course."

For good measure, she stroked his arm again. The guy about came out of his skin. He drawled, "Lloyd's, is it? Well now, little lady. I'm proper glad you're here. We'd be grateful for any help you can give us. You understand that I can only help you unofficially."

"But of course. I'd have it no other way. I'm happy to share anything I learn with you. We understand each other, then. I'll make sure my American associate behaves himself." She let a hint of disdain enter her voice as she referred to Jeff.

Thankfully, Jeff was lightning fast on the uptake and didn't react to her comment. But if she wasn't mistaken, there was a certain whiteness about his mouth—or maybe it was the clenched fists jammed deep in his pockets that gave away his tension.

She shared an overlong handshake with the eager detective, then turned to leave. She spoke to Jeff in approximately the same tone she might use to address a Great Dane. "Come along, Mr. Steiger. I need a decent cup of tea before I retire. I sincerely hope I can get one on this island."

"Along with a rousing game of cricket and some kippers," Jeff grumbled under his breath in a fake British accent.

She bit back a smile as she sailed out of the police headquarters. The car had pulled away from the curb before Jeff burst out, "Lloyd's? What if D'Abeau checks your credentials with them?"

Not going to say anything direct to her about flirting with the detective, was he? Smart man—he must realize she would call him on the little game he'd played with the woman back in the evidence locker.

"One cover story coming up." She dialed H.O.T. Watch Ops on her cell phone. "Hey, Jenn, it's Kat. I need you folks to patch a phone call through for me. Lloyd's of London. I know it doesn't open till nine London time, but they've got a twenty-four-hour number and they'll connect me to the person I need."

The H.O.T. Watch staff found the number and put the call through impressively fast. In a few moments, a woman's British-accented voice said briskly, "You're speaking to Lloyd's of London. How may I help you?"

"I need to speak to Michael Somerset. Could you ring me through to his home number straight away? Tell him it's Cobra. He'll take the call."

To the operator's credit, she didn't make any comment on the strange request. A familiar, albeit sleepy, voice came on the line.

"Cobra? What can I do for you at this lovely hour of night?"

She laughed. "I need a cover. For the next few weeks, I need to be a contract investigator for Lloyd's. Can you arrange that?"

"Sure. The boys owe me a few favors after the mess I just helped them clean up."

"You're the best."

"Anything else I can help with? Do you need any information from Lloyd's to assist in this investigation of yours?"

"Now that you mention it, I could use a list of properties in Barbados. Private homes in particular with insurable art collections."

"I assume we're talking about high-end pieces?"

"Yes."

"Do you need it now, or can I roll over and take care of it first thing in the morning?"

"Morning's soon enough."

"Is Mamba with you?" he asked hopefully.

Mamba was Medusa Aleesha Gautier's field handle. She and Michael had met and fallen in love on a mission two years ago. "Alas, no. She's still doing what she has been for the past several weeks."

"Got it."

As special operators, both of them were conditioned never to mention the specifics of any training or mission over a telephone line, secure or otherwise.

"Thanks, Michael. You're the best." She disconnected and noticed Jeff glaring over at her. "What?"

"Who in the hell is Michael Somerset?"

Amusement flashed through her. My, my. Was Mr. We've-got-to-set-this-thing-between-us-aside jealous, perchance? Apparently, after her flirting with the detective, a middle-of-the-night phone call to another man to collect a major favor was too much for Jeff to swallow.

Entertained, she shrugged. "I met Michael on a mission a couple of years back."

"And?"

She blinked innocently. "And what?"

He glared for a moment, but then, oddly, his features

smoothed out. The jealousy drained from him as quickly as it had flared. "You wouldn't be teasing me if you actually had a thing going with him."

He smiled over at her, a lopsided expression conveying chagrin. "Okay, so I deserved to have you yank my chain like that. For some inexplicable reason, I've developed a jealous streak as far as you're concerned. And no, I don't usually react this way around women. You're an anomaly. Normally, I'm the soul of nonjealousy. But then, I don't usually meet the woman I'm planning to marry, either. I plead the novelty of that event to explain my weird behavior."

He stopped babbling to shift lanes of traffic.

"Are you done yet?" she asked, now truly amused.

That earned her a baleful look.

Chuckling, she took pity and let him off the hook. "Michael helped the Medusas stop a cruise-ship hijacking. It was a dicey mission we couldn't have pulled off without him. He's British Intelligence, and he happens to be finishing up an undercover op at Lloyd's at the moment." She paused. "He's engaged to one of my teammates, if that makes you feel better."

Jeff digested that in silence for several minutes. Then he asked, "So how does it work when one of you ladies wants to get married?"

"Well, the man usually decides to pop the question, then he buys a nice engagement ring, and he thinks up some romantic and creative way to ask the Medusa in question—"

"Very funny. I'm talking about your careers."

She shrugged. "How do you guys get married and maintain your Special Forces careers?"

He frowned. "It takes a special woman to marry an operator. She has to understand the long absences, the inability to talk about our work, the psychological and emotional residue of missions…."

"It works the same for us. We have to find men with the

same qualities. Plus, they have to be okay with being around women who are a wee bit athletic and trained to do violence."

"So I gather jokes about PMS and mood swings are not recommended around y'all?"

She smiled. "Probably not at the time of the actual mood swing, no."

"Duly noted." A pause. "What about kids?"

"I'll let you know. Our team leader is pregnant right now. She's the first one of us to cross that bridge."

"Will she go back out in the field after the baby's born?"

"I don't know. The best female marathon runners in the world claim they don't reach their peak until after they've had a child. She should be able to make the physical comeback. I suppose it'll boil down to whether or not she wants to leave her baby and go back out."

"What's the military's take on it?"

"They'll work with her. They don't want to lose her."

Thankfully, the rather bizarre conversation broke off as they reached the hotel. Jeff took charge of checking them in. It was nice for a change to let someone else take the initiative and do the work. She was so used to being independent, a loner even, and to doing for herself that she almost forgot people occasionally interacted with, and even helped, each other. Her teammates aside, of course. They were family, and they all looked out for each other. It was the Medusa way.

The folks at H.O.T. Watch had arranged for a two-bedroom suite in an elegant hotel and it was ready and waiting for them. Together, she and Jeff did a routine check of the suite for bugs and cameras, and it was clean. Not that she expected otherwise. They hadn't been on the island long enough to attract that kind of attention.

When they finished, Jeff asked, "Are you up for a little field trip?"

"To the Valliard estate to figure out how the Ghost pulled off last night's heist?"

"Exactly. I thought we might indulge in a bit of breaking and entering."

She laughed up at his sparkling gaze. "How romantic. I thought you'd never ask."

"Hey, do I know how to sweep a girl off her feet or what for a second date?"

Another date? Oh, boy. They both knew it couldn't really be a date—not after their encounter in the helicopter—but even the mention of one sent her pulse racing. Meditation. She definitely needed some serious meditation. She hadn't been this jumpy and emotional since she was a kid.

She was a calm human being. Rational. In control.

And one hundred percent in lust with Jeff Steiger.

Besides kissing like a god, the man made her laugh, for crying out loud. How was she supposed to resist that?

Chapter 8

In preparation for their little field trip, Kat changed into a pair of black stretch leggings and a black turtleneck. She almost took a minute to put on a little makeup and brush her hair, until it occurred to her what she was contemplating. Disgusted with herself, she grabbed her utility belt and stuffed it into an oversize purse. Regardless of her determination not to regard this scouting mission as a date, she failed entirely to banish the thought from her mind.

They drove south from Bridgetown to the exclusive, beachfront area where the Valliard estate was located. The mansion was not visible from the road, but shielded by a thick stand of bearded ficus trees and tropical foliage. Jeff parked the car well off the road. They did a quick radio check of their headsets and mouthpieces, and then climbed out.

"I'll take point," he murmured.

They made their way swiftly through the trees. Quick electromagnetic emission scans revealed no motion sensors or cameras. The estate's security must all be concentrated up around the house. Jeff flashed her a hand signal to follow him as he made his way to the edge of the broad lawn surrounding a tall, ultramodern structure of glass and steel. Frankly, it looked like a giant, white shoebox—and was about as ugly as one.

Jeff donned a nifty set of night-vision goggles that allowed him to see infrared light, heat and even look through the home's walls. He commenced studying the estate.

"What have you got?" Kat murmured.

"Motion-sensing grid all over the lawn. A mouse couldn't get through there. I'd lay odds there are pressure sensors to match."

She gazed at the concrete walk leading up to the wide porch and its three-story-high overhang. "Is the sidewalk clean?"

Jeff studied it. "Yup. Just a sec." He adjusted his lenses. "Rotating cameras are spaced at even intervals covering the walk."

Kat looked where he pointed, and was able to pick out the small, rotating cameras. "With the right timing, those should be easy enough to slip past."

"Agreed."

"What about the house itself?"

Jeff studied the structure at some length. "I see all kinds of mechanical locks and energy sources inside the doors and windows. We're talking museum-quality security."

Her gut said the Ghost had approached the house on the sidewalk. It was certainly what she would have done. No need to take the hard way in if the easy path was wide open. As for entrance to the house itself, if the windows and doors were impenetrable, what other means could the Ghost have used to get in? She eyed the industrial-homage building. It even boasted ugly commercial air-conditioning units on the roof.

The roof. If she could get up there, she might find a way in from above. She eyed the trees on either side of the house.

Too far away to jump from one to the roof. She eyed the house itself. The Ghost might have used suction cups to scale the walls, but the rough, stucco exterior would have made using them difficult and likely would have left circular scars on the stucco. Surely Detective D'Abeau was competent enough to have spotted something that obvious.

Maybe the Ghost could've gone up one of the tall windows with the cups, but not all glass would hold an adult's weight. It would be a big risk to scale those three-story-high glass panels. How, then?

"I've got it," she announced. "I think I can get in."

"How?"

"Up the sidewalk, then up one of those porch columns. Across the roof to an air-conditioner vent and inside."

Jeff eyed the smooth concrete columns flanking the front of the house. "You couldn't climb those without damaging them. They've got no hand- or footholds. And I don't see anything at the edge of the roof that would catch and hold a grappling hook."

"I could climb one."

"Hey, I know you're a monkey, but come on. Those things are six feet across. You'd get no purchase on it. Even with a lumberjack's rig, you couldn't get enough traction with your feet to do it."

"Oh, ye of little faith. I'm telling you, I can do it."

"This I have to see."

He actually wanted her to try it? "You gonna come up on the roof with me and take a look around?"

He murmured, "I'd never ditch a lady on a date."

While she gaped at him in surprise, he added, "If you can get up there without setting off the alarms, send a rope down. I'll come up and play with you."

"Hold my gear." She stripped down to only her basic climbing equipment to reduce weight, slung a rope and cara-biners across her chest, then pulled out a small spray can.

"What's that?"

"Stickum. Athletes use it—illegally, in most cases, I might add—to make their gloves or hands sticky. Helps them make the crucial catch in the big game. Since cricket's a national obsession in Barbados and it involves catching balls, I assume this stuff's available on the island."

"Wouldn't it leave a residue on the column that the police could find?" Jeff asked.

"The good stuff that the pros sneak onto their gear evaporates quickly. Leaves practically no residue. That's how they get away with it."

Ready to leave, she paused and asked impishly, "Care to place a small wager? I say I can do it."

He grinned. "Winner gets to kiss the loser."

She laughed under her breath. No matter who won or lost, they'd get to kiss again. "You know we can't do that. Once we start, we'll never stop. How about loser pays for dinner?"

"You're on." A pause, then he added, "Chicken."

Her eyebrows shot up. "I assume you're announcing what you plan to eat, for surely you wouldn't call me that."

He grinned mischievously at her and said deliberately, "You're a chicken. Coward. Yellow belly. You're scared to kiss me again."

"And you're not scared to kiss me?"

He shrugged. "I'm willing to take my chances. I think we can be lovers and still pull off the mission. But you—you're scared of letting go. Of losing control. At the end of the day, you're more scared than I am."

Her knee-jerk reaction was to retort that she wasn't, but honesty stopped her. *Was* she that afraid to kiss him? What if she couldn't stop the next time? Then what would she do? Then she'd be in a hell of pickle, that's what. A pickle she had no intention of allowing herself to fall into, thank you very much.

Without replying to his oh-so-accurate assessment, she

took off running, skirting the edge of the lawn until she reached the sidewalk, where she crouched down. Spotting the cameras, she timed their rotation cycles and then did some quick math. In two minutes and ten seconds, they would align perfectly.

She counted down on her watch, and as the first camera swung past her, she walked quickly along behind its arc. A quick dive onto her belly as the next camera swung her way, then she was up and walking again, behind its arc. She repeated the maneuver until she stood behind one of the massive porch columns.

She pulled out a long rubber strap and passed it around the column. A quick spray of her shoes with the stickum, and she was on her way up the column. It was awkward clinging to the curving surface like a fly, but it was definitely doable. Pausing about halfway up to re-spray her shoes was tricky, but she managed.

She lunged upward with one hand to grab the edge of the roof. In the other hand, she maintained her grip on the climbing strap. For a hazardous moment, she hung precariously by her right hand, three stories above the concrete porch below. But then she flung the climbing strap around her neck and reached up with her second hand. From there, it was a piece of cake. She threw a leg up and scrambled onto the flat roof.

She ran lightly to the big air-conditioning unit, found a sturdy structural post, and attached her rope to it. Then it was back to the edge of the roof and lowering the rope until it hung a few feet above the ground. Jeff mimicked her progress up the sidewalk, then climbed the rope hand over hand quickly to join her. Dang, he'd made that look easy. Sometimes she envied the men their incredible upper-body strength.

"Now what, Spider-Woman?"

"Over here." She led him to a flat vent on the roof. "Does that caulk look fresh to you?"

Jeff knelt down beside the grate, fingering the white gel oozing out around its cracks. "Yeah. It's not entirely dry.

Smells like a liquid adhesive." He grinned up at her. "Shall we pry it up and see where it goes?"

She grinned back. Who'd have guessed breaking and entering with him would be this much fun? "After you."

"I hate to say it, but you probably ought to go first. You're so much smaller than I am; if you get stuck, we know I can't make it through. And if you do get stuck, I'll still be up here to haul you out."

"Your call, boss."

He pulled out a small crowbar and pried up the grate. The glue gave way with a moist, sucking sound. She lowered herself into the rectangular hole. After about four feet, the vertical ventilation shaft connected to a horizontal one of similar size. She eased along the low aluminum tunnel to another grate like the one above. This one showed fresh scratches in the galvanized aluminum around its screws. Yup. They'd found the Ghost's entry point.

She whispered into her microphone. "Come on down."

In a few seconds, Jeff touched her foot. "Is there room for me to slide up beside you and take a look below with my goggles before we go in?"

Kat murmured an affirmative. It was only after he'd joined her in the now very tight space, their bodies pressed against each other, rib to rib, hip to hip, with breathtaking intimacy, that it occurred to her he could've just passed the goggles forward and let her take a look around. She ought to be annoyed at him, but strangely enough, she wasn't. Such was the desperation of her craving to be near him like this. Oh, man, was she in trouble.

As they banged elbows yet again, trying to maneuver in the close confines, he whispered, "Roll on your right side."

She complied, and was stunned when he rolled onto his left side, bringing them belly to belly, chest to chest. An errant urge to ravage him right there made her freeze in shock.

"What?" he demanded. "Did you hear something?"

Yeah. Her heart about pounding out of her chest. "No, it's all clear," she replied.

"I'm going to lift the grate off and then stick my head out for a look around," he murmured.

Her nod turned into a gulp as his hard, vibrant body slid upward against hers and her nose rested somewhere in the vicinity of his zipper. Kowabunga. He made some sort of physical exertion above her head, and his body flexed unexpectedly, lurching toward the hole. She grabbed him fast, wrapping her arms around his upper thighs in case something had caused him to momentarily lose his balance.

"Give me a sec if you want more of that," he murmured. "I'll be right there."

"Are you okay?" she muttered, chagrined. "It felt like you were falling."

"I already fell for you, darlin'."

She rolled her eyes and turned his hips loose. But it wasn't like there was anywhere to retreat to. Her eyes squeezed shut in mortification, she tried to ignore the obvious view and asked in desperation, "What do you see?"

"Doesn't look like there's a stitch of security in here. Apparently, the owners relied entirely on the perimeter system."

"An expensive mistake," she replied.

"Wanna take a look around?" he asked.

"Sure. We might learn something about the Ghost."

Thankfully, his crotch finally slid past her face as he slithered through the opening and landed lightly below. She pulled herself forward with her elbows until her shoulders projected out of the opening.

"Need me to catch you?" he murmured.

By way of an answer she dived face-first through the opening, performing a neat flip in midair and landing catlike on her feet beside him. Faint moonlight from down the hall lit the startled look on his face.

She moved out silently on the balls of her feet. This was

when her traditional, soft-soled, Japanese slipper-shoes really earned their stripes. She paused before the first doorway, waiting for Jeff to join her. They fell automatically into the usual patterns of spinning low and fast past openings and leapfrogging past one another as they advanced toward the front of the house. The place was empty.

She couldn't resist showing off when they reached the stairs. A three-inch-wide stainless steel ribbon served as the handrail for the curving staircase. She leaped up onto it and ran down it, pausing only when she reached the bottom of the staircase. She stopped just short of the main floor. If the owners had any sense at all, they had pressure sensors or some sort of motion detectors down here.

Jeff looked appropriately shell-shocked when he joined her a few seconds later.

"Damn, woman. If you ever get tired of this gig, you should consider a career in the circus." He added sourly, "Please don't do that again. My heart couldn't take it."

She grinned unrepentantly at him.

Standing on the first step, he took a long look around the ground floor through the various modes of the goggles. Finally, he declared, "I can't believe it, but the ground floor's clear."

She shook her head. These people had been *asking* to be robbed. Kat looked around the expansive space. The place looked like an art gallery, with an eclectic collection of Impressionist and post-Impressionist art occupying every wall. She was no expert, but some of it looked familiar and really expensive.

"Why'd the Ghost leave all this behind?" she asked. "Why only the one painting? Once he got in here, he could've taken every last one of these works at his leisure."

Jeff frowned and moved off toward the far wall and a blue, cubist painting. Even she recognized it as a Picasso. "That's an excellent question. Particularly since I'd estimate we're looking at easily two hundred million dollars' worth of art."

She was staggered. "Really?"

Jeff nodded grimly as he examined a painting closely. "This Picasso is probably more valuable than the Monet that the Ghost took."

"Sounds like our guy's stealing on commission then. He's not going after random art to pawn. He's stealing specific pieces for a collector."

Jeff moved away from the Picasso and stood back to look at a large Impressionist scene of water and boats. "No doubt about it."

She commented lightly, "Good thing we're on the right side of the law. Between the two of us, we could make a fortune nicking this stuff."

He grunted. "This one job would set us up for life."

They traded knowing looks. Temptations like this weren't uncommon in their line of work. However, it was the rare operator who crossed the line, and neither of them were of that weak-willed ilk.

She asked, "Now what? You wanna climb back out of here, or should we make a phone call to Detective D'Abeau and give him heart failure?"

Jeff grinned. "The guy could use a good heart attack. Serve him right for flirting with you the way he did."

"He wouldn't be amused," she warned.

"Yeah, you're right," Jeff replied reluctantly.

She followed him back upstairs, using the actual steps this time. They reached the air vent and she looked up at it. "If I were the Ghost, I'd have left a rope hanging here to climb out on," she remarked as she hoisted herself back into the vent.

"Now that you mention it, there's a rounded dent in that far corner of the vent opening," Jeff commented. "Like a rope would make if a lot of weight were put on it."

"Good eye," she replied. Jeff nodded, acknowledging the compliment as she asked, "Need a hand up?"

"Nah."

He showed off a bit himself by jumping and grabbing the lip of the opening. While hanging there, he curled up in a ball and then shot his feet up and forward through the opening. As intellectually advanced as she might consider herself, a primitive part of her still thrilled at the masculine display of strength. Yup, she was officially a mess.

They crawled back out onto the roof and re-secured the vent cover before easing over to the edge of the roof. From there it was an easy matter to retrace their route down to the porch, down the sidewalk between the cameras, and back out to their car.

They reached their hotel room slightly before dawn and retired to their respective beds quickly. It felt exceedingly strange, knowing that Jeff was sleeping so nearby, enjoying the hotel's six-hundred-thread-count Egyptian cotton sheets against his skin the same way she was. Eventually, she resorted to a self-hypnosis exercise and managed to put herself to sleep, but it wasn't an easy thing. Memories of sapphire eyes and a vibrant male body pressing intimately against hers kept interrupting her best efforts to clear her mind.

A delicious smell of freshly fried bacon woke her up the next morning. She opened her eyes and jolted to see Jeff standing beside her bed, smiling down at her.

"Good morning, beautiful."

Oh, crap. Pajama check. Thank God she'd pulled on a sloppy cotton T-shirt last night and not the whisper-thin silk nightshirt she usually favored. "Uh, hi." She pushed her hair out of her face and rubbed her eyes. "What are you doing here?"

"I brought my favorite cat burglar breakfast in bed."

She sat up, propping several pillows behind her back. He set a lap tray across her legs, and she stared down at steak, fried eggs, stewed tomatoes, bacon, a stack of pancakes, and half a red grapefruit. "I couldn't eat all of this in a week of breakfasts!"

He shrugged. "I didn't know what you'd like, so I ordered a variety."

"Have you eaten yet?" She picked up a spoon and dug into the juicy grapefruit.

"Heavens, no. My grandmère taught me that a gentleman always feeds his lady first."

"You know, I think I'm starting to like your grandmère."

His eyes clouded over. "Too bad you can't meet her. She passed away a few years back. Cancer."

Quick sympathy speared through her. She knew how bad it hurt to lose a beloved anchor in one's life. "I'm sorry."

He shrugged, but there was old pain in the gesture. He changed subjects abruptly, and she went with the flow in total understanding. "Here's the morning newspaper. You and I managed to stay out of it."

"Thank goodness. That's the last thing we need." She dug into the fried eggs and pushed him the stack of pancakes.

She watched, appalled, while he drowned the flapjacks in syrup.

As he cut into them, he asked, "So where'd the Ghost get the stickum he used to climb the column? Yours came in an aerosol can. If he flew to Barbados, he couldn't have brought it with him. So where on the island did he pick it up?"

She shrugged. "A sporting goods store, probably."

"Can't be too many of those on this island. Think it's worth tracking down?"

"Our particular talents are probably better used elsewhere. Why don't I mention it to Detective D'Abeau? He's got plenty of manpower to check it out, and he'd love to hear from me again," she said lightly.

A black look flitted across Jeff's gaze, but to his credit, he made no comment.

Feeling a little guilty for the poke, she said quickly, "What are the odds that we can guess where the Ghost will strike next? I'm not fond of always being one step behind the guy like this. I'd rather be waiting for him at his next hit."

Jeff opened his mouth to reply, but a knock on the hallway door startled them just then, and he was out of the room before she could blink. She leaped out of bed and threw on pants, grabbing a pistol and sliding toward her bedroom door on bare feet.

"You can come out," Jeff called. "The hotel had some faxes to deliver."

She didn't question the fact that he knew to tell her to stand down. He'd assumed she would cover his back, and he'd assumed correctly. She stowed the pistol in the holster sewn in the back waistband of her slacks and stepped out into the sunny living room. "Who're the faxes from?"

"Lloyd's of London sent you a pile of stuff. And there's one here from Viper—unless you know anyone else who signs their notes, *V*."

She scanned Viper's fax quickly. "The supercomputer came up with a catalog called 'Undiscovered Masterpieces of the Great Artists,' published last year. All the paintings stolen so far have been in it."

Jeff gaped. "No kidding?"

She passed him the paper. "Vanessa says she's contacted someone who's going to send a copy of the catalog to her. She'll scan it and send us the file as soon as she gets it."

He nodded slowly. "The Ghost's employer isn't an art connoisseur if he's using a catalog to identify what constitutes great art. Which means any rich bastard in the world could be our guy. I was really hoping a sophisticated trend would emerge in the collector's taste. It would narrow the suspect list considerably."

His logic sounded on target. Which meant they couldn't go through the Ghost's client to get at the thief. They'd have to catch the guy directly.

Jeff was flipping through the second sheaf of papers, the ones from Lloyd's. "If we can get a hold of that catalog, we can check it against this list of insured art on the island and see if any more of the paintings in it are here in Barbados. Your friend Michael didn't only send us Lloyd's list of insured art, here. It looks like his buddies at Lloyd's called all the other major insurers of art worldwide and compiled their lists of insured pieces in Barbados, too."

"Gotta love that British efficiency."

He grinned. "Yeah. And friends in high places."

"Amen. So. With that list in hand, do you think we can predict the next piece the Ghost might go after?"

"It's worth a shot."

Kat's PDA beeped distinctively on her nightstand. "That's the incoming e-mail signal. Maybe that's the catalog now." She dashed into the bedroom to check. "Yup, it's the file." Jeff hurried after her, and they huddled over the handheld device as the pages of the catalog scrolled across its tiny screen.

She was *not* paying attention to the fact that she and Jeff were sitting on the side of the same bed. She was *not* imagining falling backward across it, their limbs tangled in naked abandon while they made passionate love with each other. She hardly saw the paintings go scrolling by, so vividly aware was she of Jeff only inches away from her, smelling like expensive shampoo and subtle aftershave. He smelled good enough to eat. She probably smelled like the sour sweat of last night's exertions, and her hair was no doubt sticking up all over her head like broom straw.

She mumbled, "Mind if I jump in the shower while you compare this catalog to the list of pieces here on the island?"

Such was Jeff's concentration on the incoming file that he barely acknowledged her as she slipped out of the room. Or maybe he was just covering up being as flustered as she was. She hoped the latter was the case.

When she stepped out of the bathroom a half hour later,

wearing form-fitting white yoga pants and a matching tank top, lotioned, powdered, perfumed and primped within an inch of her life, Jeff looked up from the papers…and stopped cold.

"Wow. You look fantastic."

She smiled even as she mentally shook her head at her absurdly pleased reaction to the compliment. She had to admit, having him around did wonders for her ego. "Any matches?"

"Yes. Several. What say for our third date we stake out a ghost? I'll even throw in a picnic."

Another date. Complete with the close quarters and adrenaline rush of a stakeout? And food, no less? How could a girl say no to that? Her mouth curved up into a smile. "I had no idea that running a Special Ops mission could be so civilized. We Medusas have obviously been doing it all wrong."

"Obviously." His dimples flashed and her knees went weak on cue. "Stick with me, babe. I'll show you the ropes."

"Or maybe I'll show you how it's done, big guy."

His dancing gaze met hers. "We haven't even begun to have fun yet, darlin'."

Chapter 9

From the catalog, Jeff picked out the likeliest painting of the three that were still left to steal here in Barbados, and he and Kat obtained grudging permission from Detective D'Abeau to stake it out. But after Kat had advanced a plausible "theory" of how the Ghost had gained entrance to the Valliard estate, the cop had owed her one. Not to mention that she'd flirted with him some more. The memory of her casting come-hither looks at that cop continued to set Jeff's teeth on edge. It might be just business, but he still didn't like it.

Kat's buddy in London had sent them the house layouts and security plans of the likely target, along with a note that of the three properties they'd identified as being probable targets, this one had the least extensive security system. If the Ghost was going to strike again, Jeff was betting they'd pegged his next mark correctly.

He and Kat spent all afternoon poring over the house plans and wiring diagrams, planning how they'd rob the place if they were the Ghost. Anticipation at the idea of nabbing the bastard made Jeff edgy. His tension had nothing to do with the mesmerizing woman leaning over the drawings across from him, giving him tantalizingly incomplete glimpses down her shirt of small but perfect breasts that his hands itched to touch and his mouth itched to taste. He was a cad to look, but his gaze broke completely out of his control every time she leaned across the table just so.

This mansion, a sprawling one-story affair unoriginally called Shangri-La, had copious security measures inside the house as well as out. Kat suggested several outrageous methods of bypassing the system…things even an acrobat of her caliber would surely not be able to pull off.

But when he challenged her on it, she casually claimed she could do everything she was suggesting. And somehow, he believed her. He'd about passed out when she took off down that railing last night. She'd looked like a circus performer running along a tightrope. He'd never met another operator who could do some of the things she could. And damn if his imagination didn't keep straying to adventurous things he'd love to try with her in bed that took advantage of her athleticism and flexibility.

After hours of brainstorming together, they arrived at the conclusion that the Ghost would have to disable the entire security system, or simply set it off and move in fast to make the hit and leave before the police arrived. And, frankly, if there was a way to turn off the security system and not have the police know about it instantly, the two of them couldn't find it.

Which was outstanding news for them. If the Ghost were operating in a two- or three-minute window to get in and get out, they reasoned he'd have to eschew fancy circus maneuvers and just make a fast grab at the painting in question. Which also meant they stood a decent chance of nabbing the guy.

Jeff was exultant. Finally, the setup he'd been waiting for to move in and catch this bastard.

Ideally, they'd be inside the mansion for this stakeout, but the Bajan police didn't trust them that much, flirting or no. And frankly, neither he nor Kat wanted the exposure to suspicion if something went wrong and the Ghost got away. In that event, they'd be left as the only people known to have been inside the house when the painting went missing.

The painting was one of Turner's smaller landscapes, a brilliant piece. If Jeff were an art collector with ten million bucks burning a hole in his pocket, he'd snap it up in a heartbeat. The art catalog Viper had sent them raved about the piece, claiming it was one of the finest privately owned landscapes in the world. Oh yeah. Their greedy collector wouldn't be able to resist this tasty morsel.

Jeff retired to take a nap before the night's festivities began. He slept restlessly, dreaming of dark eyes and ivory skin and silky black hair falling down around him. That girl was a fever in his blood. He thought about her constantly, and none of his thoughts were platonic in nature. How in hell he was going to keep his hands off her for days or weeks to come, he hadn't the faintest idea. And he suspected this torturous itch would get a whole lot worse before it got better. He wanted her worse than any woman he'd ever laid eyes on.

When he finally got up and went out into the living room, he was startled by the sight that greeted him. Kat had pushed all the furniture back to the walls, and was in the midst of performing a complex and insanely difficult martial arts routine. Oh, Lord. And now he had these images to add to his fantasies of her. The thought of what they could do with a few of her contortions plumb stole his breath away.

He didn't know whether to be grateful or dismayed when she caught sight of him and froze. He mumbled, "Don't stop on my account."

"It's okay. I just needed to clear my mind."

He nodded in understanding. "Sweat does wonders for my thought processes, too." He moved over to the sofa, which was now tucked underneath the window, and flopped down on it. "What style of martial art was that you were practicing?"

"It's a hybrid form. Part judo. Part kung fu. Part...other stuff."

"What other stuff?"

She frowned. "Just stuff Hidoshi-san showed me. I don't know where he got it from."

"Liar."

He said the word so calmly it seemed to take Kat a moment to register it. Then she whirled to face him, staring.

He explained, "You've studied your whole life, or darned near all of it, to have achieved your level of proficiency. You're not some casual hobbyist, you're a martial arts master. And every practitioner with your level of dedication knows the pedigree and sources of his art back as far as it goes."

"You overestimate my skill."

"My dear, I think not only I, but also the United States government, have grossly *under*estimated your skill. Do General Wittenauer or your teammates have any idea what you can really do?"

"Why do you ask such a thing?" she asked sharply.

"Because if anybody knew what you're capable of, you'd be famous in the Spec Ops community. Hell, you'd be a legend."

Something approaching panic flitted across her face. "Nobody must know," she choked out.

"Why not? Why not shout to the heavens about your abilities? Do you have any idea the things you could do for our country?"

Panic flashed openly in her gaze now.

"My vow—" She broke off.

"What vow?"

She shook her head quickly. "I mustn't speak of it."

"Let me guess. Hidoshi-san taught you the ancient family

fighting form. You're sworn to silence and mustn't ever reveal the family secrets."

"Close enough," she replied reluctantly.

"And it's only to be shared with blood relatives."

That caused a pained look to cross her face, but she made no reply.

"Your secret's safe with me, darlin'. After all, we're practically family already. Once we're married, will you be able to teach it to me? I'd love to learn some of what you can do."

She burst out, "Will you *stop* talking like that?"

He surged to his feet and closed the space between them quickly. "I'm serious, Kat. I want you and I'm going to have you. I've never met another woman like you. Cupid's Bolt or not, I'd still go after you full bore."

She stared up at him in wide-eyed disbelief.

Irritation flooded through him. "What's so damn hard to believe about that?"

She just shook her head.

Throwing caution to the winds, he grabbed her shoulders in both hands. Thankfully, she didn't toss him to the floor. He asked low and furiously, "Why won't you believe me?"

"I don't…I can't…"

"Can't what? Can't talk to me? Can't tell me how you feel or what you're thinking? Can't—or won't, Kat? I'm sick to death of this strong, silent act of yours."

Her mouth quirked wryly. "I thought that was usually the girl's line."

"Hah. You're the ninja in this relationship."

Kat went completely still. Horror flowed through her and into his hands. *What the—*

He burst out, "Oh, God. A *ninja?* Is that what your grandfather trained you to be?" It made perfect sense. The acrobatic things he'd seen her do…the amazing fighting skills… the crazy climbing ability… He swore again under his breath.

It was her turn to grab him by the arms. "Nobody must know, Jeff. *Nobody*."

"Why not? My God, think of the training you could give our Special Forces—"

"But that's the point. That's not how it's done. I can't pick and choose cool pieces of the Way and share them with outsiders. There's a code…consequences."

He studied her intently. "You're really worried about this. Is there some super-secret ninja society that'll come and get you if you give away their secrets?"

Momentary humor flickered in her eyes. "No, nothing like that. But I took a solemn vow. I *can't* break it. It would dishonor Hidoshi-san's memory." She threw up her hands. "I know to a Westerner that sounds completely lame. But it's a big deal to me."

He captured her restless hands and drew them against his chest. "It doesn't sound lame to me. Hey, I'm a soldier, too. Honor counts in my world. Promises matter to me. I get it."

She blinked up at him, suddenly still. "Do you mean that?"

He frowned. "Yes, I mean it. If you don't want me to tell anyone about your training, I won't."

"Just like that?"

He flung her hands away from him and turned to pace the room. "Why do you always question everything I say? Why can't you accept that I stand by my word? Are we Westerners that weak and untrustworthy in your eyes?"

"I… You… No…"

He stopped prowling and crossed his arms over his chest as she sputtered to a stop. "Darlin', that was not the most convincing denial I've ever heard."

She huffed. "Fine. I admit it. I don't generally think too highly of Western promises."

Ouch. He had to give her credit, though. She didn't flinch from speaking the truth. "What about your teammates? These Medusas you speak so highly of? Do you trust them?"

That got a rise out of her. Oh, she didn't stomp or yell or anything so crass, but abrupt anger rolled off her. Only a faint tightness in her voice betrayed her irritation. "I trust them with my life."

Such control she had. Were it not for the inexplicable, but very real, connection between the two of them, he doubted he'd have had any clue she was so pissed off at the moment.

He asked reasonably, "Why them and not me? Is it because you and I haven't come under hostile fire together yet? Do I need to take you out with my team the next time we take a stroll through hell to gain your trust?"

Her forehead twitched, but she never actually frowned. He waited her out while she mulled over his question. Finally, she replied, "You would have had to have been there when the Medusas formed to understand. The powers that be did everything they could to make us fail. The only reason we made it through our initial training is because we all—every one of us Medusas—committed everything we had to each other."

He nodded in total comprehension. An operator's team was much more than a bunch of coworkers. More than family, even. Facing death together time and again forged a bond unlike anything else. It went way beyond words.

He asked matter-of-factly, "You've worked with other special operators, haven't you? Men, yes? Do you trust them? Or is it something special about me that causes you not to trust me?"

She sighed. "I do trust you."

"But not enough to believe what I say."

Her face went expressionless, her voice flat. "Why are you pushing this argument?"

She was pulling back from him. Again. Every time they approached a truly intimate moment, physical or emotional, she backed away like a big dog. Enough was enough. He wasn't going to stand by and let it happen again.

He stepped into her personal space until she leaned away

from him uncomfortably, and spoke silkily. "Am I making you mad, Kat? Is that why you're shutting down on me? More of that stoic Eastern fatalism you're so proud of?"

"Fatalism?" she echoed ominously.

"Yeah. And it's a load of crap, by the way."

He all but saw her hackles rise at that. "Emotional control is all well and good. But there's a time and place for it. I thought balance was part of your precious Eastern philosophy. Where's the balance in never allowing yourself to feel a damn thing?"

"I feel things," she said, flaring.

Ahh. Better. "Right," he grunted skeptically. "That's why you always run and hide behind your superhuman self-control. Because you're so busy feeling stuff."

Her voice was very nearly snippy when she retorted, "Just because I choose not to wear my every thought or feeling on my sleeve doesn't make me overcontrolled. If you want to live your entire life as a wide-open book for any old passerby to see, that's your choice. But it doesn't make my choice wrong."

He allowed himself a smile at that not-so-subtle jab. Finally. He'd gotten a visible rise out of her. "Very good, Kat," he said approvingly. "You're learning. Now if we can just get you to shout now and then, you'll be on your way to a healthier balance in your life."

She stared at him, clearly surprised out of her snit.

"Honey, you're not the only one who can mask feelings and motives. Just because I choose to express mine honestly and openly to you doesn't mean I'm not capable of reining them in or disguising them outright."

"So you set out deliberately to make me angry?" she asked, dangerously softly.

Instinct screamed at him to beat a hasty retreat from this lethal woman. Instead, he shrugged with what he hoped was enough arrogance to really tick her off. "What of it?"

Even though he expected the move, when she leaped at him, it happened so fast he had no chance whatsoever to react. Even if he had managed to throw up a block in time, he wouldn't have done it today. If it took letting her knock his head off to get her to open up to him, so be it.

Her foot flew past his nose so close that he actually felt the faintest brush of it on his skin, as light as butterfly wings, but deadly in its explosive power. The edge of her hand, as stiff as a knife blade, stopped a millimeter from his neck. He dared to glance down and saw her other fist poised in front of his sternum, stopped midblow in a strike that would have crushed it like glass.

He looked up, capturing her furious gaze. He asked much more calmly than he felt, "Why didn't you hurt me?"

Frustration seeped into her eyes.

"Go ahead. Say it," he challenged.

Still the silent war within her raged, a lifetime's worth of repressing thoughts and feelings winning out over what he knew she really wanted to say and do.

"Need me to help you?"

She opened her mouth but no words came out.

He reached out and wrapped her, lethal hands and all, in his arms, dragging her up roughly against him. He kissed her then, holding nothing back. She was too angry for finesse, too wrapped up in her repressed rage for anything other than extreme measures to register. Kissing an enraged woman wasn't his first choice in self-preservation, but if it was what she needed, he'd take his chances.

There was nothing elegant about their kiss. He flattened her lips against her teeth as she fought him, flatly insisting that she acknowledge and react to him. She tried to hold out, but he tightened his grip on her, forcing her body to arch backward beneath his onslaught.

She fought, but not with real intent to harm him. She could've just as easily bitten his lip, kneed him in the groin, or executed a dozen other moves to incapacitate him. And yet, she did none of those things. As he'd thought. She wanted him to force her out of her emotional shell. And he was good and ready to have her emerge from it himself. She tested his strength, trying to pull out of his arms, and he obliged her by engaging his superior strength to hold her right there against him.

In spite of their wrestling embrace, he couldn't help but register that she tasted like plums, rich and sweet and tangy. Her mouth was ripe and juicy, and he devoured her hungrily, sucking in the taste of her, drawing her into him until she became a part of him. He'd love to gentle the kiss, to savor the rich taste of her, to enjoy her languidly and completely.

But first, he wanted all of her—no reservations. He felt the piece she was holding back. It dangled tantalizingly, just beyond his reach. But he also felt her control of that piece of herself slipping.

He schooled himself to patience, following through on the forceful embrace cautiously, making dead sure not to lose himself in the violence of the moment. He would never, ever attack a woman in anger, particularly with a strong sexual element in the mix. He might be forcing the issue, but he refused to force the woman.

Finally, she tore her mouth away from his, swearing in several languages he did recognize and a couple he didn't. "You're a beast," she hissed.

He maintained his grip on her, keeping her arms safely pinned between them. After all, he wasn't a complete fool, and she was still one very pissed off ninja at the moment.

"Passion is not bestiality, Katrina. Nor is it lack of control. If I had no control, you'd be on the floor right now beneath me while I had at you like a true beast. Like it or not, darlin', I'm bigger and stronger than you are. You might be a ninja, but I've got you in a position where I can outmuscle you. And yet, I'm not mauling you, nor am I falling upon you mindlessly. This is about *you* letting go—not me."

She still vibrated with anger, but her explosive readiness to do violence seemed to diminish slightly.

He spoke gently then, silken strands of her hair lightly caressing his lips. "Human emotions are not bad things. In fact, they can be wonderful things. Why do you deny yourself pleasure—hell, real happiness—like this? Surely, your grandfather didn't want that for you."

More of the tension drained from her, replaced by something else he recognized very well indeed. A humming sexual awareness of him, of her body, of how he made her feel. Nonetheless, he didn't loosen his grip quite yet. After all, deception was part of both their training.

"Give it a try," he murmured. "Let go. Allow yourself to really feel something. Just for a minute or two. It'll be our secret, like your ninja training."

When she still hesitated, he took a mental deep breath and made an enormous leap of faith. He turned her loose.

She stood there for a second, gazing up at him, her fists resting lightly on his chest, her body so close to his he felt her warmth radiating through their clothes.

Had he blown it? Would she turn away from him now and never look back? Or kill him, perhaps? He had no doubt she could do it with her bare hands. And he didn't have it in him to stop her if she tried. He could never hurt her that way.

Lord, he felt exposed. Like he was standing in front of a firing squad.

And then her hands moved slightly on his chest, her fingers splaying open gradually until her palms rested against him, warm through his shirt. Her hands slid so slowly, and he held his breath, not sure if he was experiencing a miracle or slow-motion murder.

She swayed slightly toward him. He could swear that was wonderment dawning in her eyes. He stood perfectly still, letting her do whatever she liked to him. Thus encouraged, her hands strayed from his shoulders to his face, her finger-tips lightly tracing his cheekbones, the line of his jaw, his mouth.

"You're beautiful," she whispered.

His eyes widened. Could it be?

Slowly, she rose up on tiptoe, leaning lightly against him. Her right hand went around the back of his neck and tugged lightly. He bent his head down for her, never breaking eye contact with her as she raised her mouth by slow degrees to his.

Their lips touched.

Where before they'd met in violence, this time they came together with the lightest of touches, igniting an aching ardor in his soul that was unlike anything he'd ever experienced. This transcended lust, went beyond simple pleasure. It was as if something sacred and rare were unfolding within his soul.

All from the barest touch of her lips to his?

Maybe there was something to this Eastern control stuff after all.

Kat stepped back. "There," she murmured. "That's a proper beginning between us."

Chapter 10

Shangri-La and its tempting Turner landscape were about a mile from the Valliard place on the same stretch of mansion-strewn beach. In daylight, the house—almost a parody of island architecture—would be a tacky flamingo color, with white plantation shutters galore. Tonight it was faintly peach in the moonlight. Kat studied the gaudy architecture and had to shake her head that anyone would build, let alone live in, something so garish.

She and Jeff had chosen to approach the mansion from the beach in extreme stealth, on the off chance that the Ghost was lurking nearby, casing the place. Hence, the two of them were crammed side by side in a hollow beneath a cluster of sharp-leaved palmettos, incidentally exchanging more information about their anatomies than she'd ever imagined possible completely clothed. Who'd have guessed a guy's deltoids flexed like that when he propped a pair of binoculars in front of his nose? Or that a man's thigh went quite that hard when a girl had to drape her leg over it while reaching into her waist pouch to retrieve a lens attachment for her surveillance camera.

"Having fun yet?" Jeff murmured.

Fun? This was like having a root canal without painkillers. It was so much easier to be out in the field with a bunch of women. None of these errant thoughts and sensations distracted her from the job at hand. Except she'd worked with men before, and this had never been a problem. It was definitely Jeff who messed her up like this.

Was he right? Was her life out of balance because it lacked real emotion?

Belatedly, she responded to his question in an undertone that wouldn't carry more than a few feet. "I wouldn't go so far as to call this fun. I feel naked without my sniper rig."

He laughed under his breath. "Now there's a line I've never heard on a date before. What's the longest shot you've ever made?"

"Confirmed kill?"

"Yeah."

"About thirteen hundred yards. But I mostly do short-range work."

"Who's the most famous person you've taken out?"

She looked over at him askance. "You keep score of such things?"

He grinned. "I've never been out on a date with a sniper. I'm not exactly sure how to engage in small talk with you."

"Well, what do you talk about with the other women you date?"

"Ahh, darlin'. We don't usually get around to doing much talking."

If he'd had his night-vision goggles on at that moment, her face would have lit up bright white with embarrassed heat. And it obviously amused him. The cad.

He asked, "Don't you ever feel like blowing off steam after a mission? A little hot, meaningless sex for the hell of it?"

Sex? Her? Not so much. It was too overwhelming. Too personal. Okay, fine. Too emotional. She replied dryly, "I go to the dojo and get in a hard workout if I need to burn off adrenaline. But usually I go someplace peaceful and green to meditate for a while."

He tsked. "You don't know what you're missing out on. Adrenaline-pumped sex is incredible. You should try it sometime."

She just shook her head. She could not believe she was out on a stakeout and having this conversation.

He continued, "When I come off a tough mission, I want to do something mindless and physical to remind myself that I'm still alive. I don't know any guy who doesn't want sex right after he came off a rough op. Maybe it's a guy-girl difference." He paused, then added, "Do all the Medusas meditate after missions?"

Kat suppressed a startled sound of laughter. "Not hardly. They go out and party. Or nowadays, they go home to their guys. I'm the only bachelor left in the bunch."

"Why do you meditate instead of partying?"

"After I make a kill, I usually feel a need to re-center myself."

Sounding mildly alarmed, he asked, "You don't take kills personally, do you?"

"Not at all. If I didn't do it, someone else would. I'm just the tool that carries out a decision made way above my pay grade."

"What about when a mission goes to hell and you end up unexpectedly having to shoot your way out? Or hasn't that happened to the Medusas?"

She answered wryly, "It's happened more than once. Then it's even simpler. In that scenario, it's kill or be killed. You pull the trigger and you don't think twice. I never look back from those kills."

"I've got to say, I never thought a woman could take such a broad view of killing. I always assumed women wouldn't get it."

"You think we're all wilting lilies who wring our hands over squishing a bug and have to ask a man to do it for us?"

He laughed under his breath. "Are you kidding? I've read my history. Some of the most violent soldiers in history have been women. Did you ever hear what Russian women did to German prisoners of war in World War II? It's no wonder the Germans always saved one bullet for themselves."

Kat was familiar with the Russian women's practice of tying enemy soldiers to trees and whipping them until their innards wrapped around the trunk. Although after what the Nazis had done to the Soviet Union, she couldn't blame the women for their rage.

She murmured, "Surely you talk with women a little bit about something besides killing when you're out on a date with one. You know, normal stuff."

She hoped she didn't sound like she was fishing to find out what normal was. Even if that was exactly what she was doing. Jeff countered with, "What did you talk about on dates with boys when you were in high school or college?"

"I didn't date in high school. Hidoshi-san didn't pass away until I was seventeen. When I came to the States to go to college, I was so busy trying to bring my English up to speed and keep my grades up and adjust to the culture shock that I didn't have much time for a social life." And the few relationships she'd had with college boys had left her unimpressed with dating in general. The guys she'd gone out with didn't have a fraction of her focus or drive, and she'd found them…frivolous.

"Why didn't Hidoshi-san let you date?"

"Oh, he'd have let me date. But I was too busy training to spare the time for such silliness."

"Wow. You must have been one mega-serious teenager." He grinned over at her self-deprecatingly. "The same could not have been said about me. My high school teachers always harped at me about applying myself more. About all I applied myself to back then were sports and girls. And not necessarily in that order."

She didn't find that hard to believe. And yet, when the two of them had talked through possible plans for catching the Ghost, he was as focused as any operator she'd ever worked with. He seemed to subscribe to the theory of working hard and playing hard in about equal measure.

He asked, "Were you always so committed to your martial arts, even at a young age?"

"I started training when I could barely walk. I've done it hard-core my entire life. It's who I am."

"That's a strong statement."

"If you're so determined to pursue a relationship with me, you need to believe me. My training runs bone deep. The physical aspects, the mental aspects, the ancient code of honor—all of it."

"Why did you choose the martial arts as your framework for self-definition?"

She turned her head to stare at him.

He shrugged. "So, sue me. I was a psychology minor in college."

Great. She'd fallen for an amateur shrink. She sure could pick 'em. His question was insightful, though. She finally murmured, "I had nothing else. No one else. Hidoshi-san loved me when no one else did. Becoming like him was the least I could do to show my gratitude."

"No one else loved you? The absentee father, I understand. But what about siblings? Aunts and uncles?"

"Nada."

He shifted the weight off one elbow and reached out to touch her cheek. Just the slightest graze of his fingertips against her skin. "Are you still completely alone?"

The loneliness aching within her radiated outward in a terrible tension that froze her facial muscles beneath his brief touch. Her entire being felt stiff as she answered, "I have the Medusas now. They're my family."

He nodded as if he knew the feeling well. And, given that he had a team of his own that he ran with, he probably did know the feeling. "But what about you? Isn't there anyone in your life just for you?"

"Is all this psychoanalysis really necessary?" she asked lightly.

"You're avoiding the question. Your grandfather has passed away, and you have no one else, do you?"

He was prodding painful places in her soul that she'd just as soon have him leave alone. She retreated into the emotionless cool she always did when people tried to get too close to her. Except this time, she felt like a coward for running away. Damn him! She'd been happy the way she was before she met him...or at least at peace with herself. Why did he have to go and tear away the veil of her lonely existence like that and show it to her for what it really was?

She answered in a tone that sounded stilted, even to her. "I don't need anyone else, so your question is moot."

He nodded sagely. "The lady has built her very own fortress of solitude. And here you were, doing so well at starting to crawl out of it. I'm a pushy jerk, aren't I?"

Secretly relieved that he'd poked at her—given her an excuse to come out of her emotional cave, really—she rolled her eyes. "You got one part right. You are a jerk." But she said it without any real heat.

He grinned over at her. "And you love me anyway."

Stunned, she jerked her gaze back to the estate in front of her while she turned the concept over in her mind. Did she feel love for him? Was it possible? She'd loved Hidoshi. But that was different. She'd loved him as a child loves a parent or grandparent.

But Jeff? Could she love a man like him? As an equal? A mate? She stared fixedly through her spotter's scope, seeing a blurry morass of green and peach, vividly aware that he was studying her in the meantime.

"Dare I hope?" he breathed. "Are there really feelings for me lurking behind that inscrutable exterior of yours?"

She started to lower the fist-size telescope to glare over at him, but something caught her attention at the farthest edge of her vision, and she jerked the scope back up to her eye. "I've got movement," she announced. "I do believe our Ghost is putting in an appearance."

Jeff lurched, his attention swinging back to the mansion. "Say position," he responded tersely, abruptly back in full mission mode.

"Eleven o'clock. North end of the upper terrace. Moving in low and fast toward the shed housing the main electrical boxes."

They'd been right, then. The Ghost was simply going to knock out the alarm and make a speed run for the painting. Earlier, they'd discussed trying to nab the guy as soon as they spotted him or waiting until he'd stolen the painting and then catching him. Their concern was that if they grabbed him before the theft, the police wouldn't have enough evidence to hold the guy. He'd slip away from them, this time for good.

"Good eye," Jeff murmured. "He's practically invisible."

"I should think any respectable thief is invisible most of the time," she murmured back absently, concentrating hard on not losing sight of the elusive figure. Likewise, any half-decent sniper ought to be able to follow a figure like him at this distance. And she was more than half decent.

Jeff breathed, "Let's move in closer. Full stealth. We don't want to spook this guy."

She nodded, rising silently to a crouch and easing off through the imitation Balinese landscaping behind Jeff. She didn't hear a sound as they slipped through the night. Jeff was every bit as good as she was at this silent sneaking thing—and she'd been trained by the best. Hidoshi had been one of the last great ninja masters.

Jeff hand-signaled her to go around the house and watch the front doors while he took the oceanside doors. She nodded and Jeff hand-signaled. "First one to spot him leaving calls for backup. Then we move in on him."

She nodded and glided off into the dark, at one with the night. Adrenaline sang through her veins and her body was light and responsive. She was ready for whatever came. Moments like this, where she got to fully turn her skills loose, were rare. But in these moments she was profoundly grateful to Hidoshi, to whatever quirk of fate had led her to him, that she'd been granted the opportunity to do this. To be this.

Jeff found a carved tiki pole casting a deep shadow and had just taken up position behind it when every light in the mansion abruptly came on and a piercing noise split the night.

"Time hack," he announced. He looked down at his watch. Three-twenty a.m. on the nose. He figured they had about sixty seconds to wait, and then one of them should spot the Ghost leaving with his prize. He scanned the ground-floor doors and windows on this side of the house, watching for the slightest movement anywhere in his field of vision.

Eighty-two seconds had passed since his time hack when two things happened simultaneously. He heard the first police sirens in the far distance, and Kat radioed, "I've got him. He's coming out the front door now."

"Go get him!" Jeff ordered as he took off sprinting around the house.

And then all hell broke loose.

No less than five heavily armed men burst out of the bushes in front of Jeff, forcing him to screech to a halt and drop to the ground. "Incoming!" he whispered urgently to Kat. "Five armed men heading your way. Might be cops. Hold your fire!"

The men charged forward away from his position—toward Kat and the Ghost. A spurt of panic broadsided him. Those guys were headed straight at Kat! He briefly considered standing up and shouting at the men to draw their attention and their fire away from her. But then his brain kicked back into gear. She was a trained Special Forces operative. She knew what to do when a bunch of guys ran in her general direction.

As the men moved away, Jeff ran lightly behind them, staying well out of their line of sight and possible line of fire. Who *were* these guys? If they were police, they were certainly acting weird. Cops would have shouted for the Ghost to halt, would have fired warning shots in the air. Searchlights would flare to life, rows of police cars would shine their headlights, and the Ghost would be well and truly caught.

But these guys were sprinting grimly, pistols at the ready, silent, coordinated, and for all the world moving like a team of commandos closing in for a kill.

He careened around the side of the house and spied the front door gaping wide open. One of the men was just leaving the front porch to rejoin his buddies. Jeff ducked behind a lush hibiscus as the guy raced past him. The guy was wearing a black knit cap and black greasepaint on his face. SWAT team maybe, but no regular cop dressed like that.

Jeff risked whispering to Kat, "Where are you?"

"Running," she grunted.

As a powerful engine gunned nearby, the men dropped any attempt at stealth and took off running, yelling back and forth in what sounded like something Slavic.

"Cobra! Five targets straight at you!" Jeff called urgently. He swore violently as the team of armed men sprinted right at Kat. He was too far away to fling himself in front of her but, had he been beside her, he'd have done it in a heartbeat.

She veered off to the right, smartly separating herself from the Ghost as a target. The bad guys lurched and slowed momentarily in their surprise at spotting her. But now they had her in their sights and seemed determined to bag her, too. Three men peeled off after the Ghost; the other two went after her.

It was a no-brainer which group he was going after. No way was he leaving her alone to face down these guys on her own.

Neither he nor Kat was heavily armed. Without knowing how skilled—or unskilled—these guys were, he dared not take them on directly in any kind of a fight. Besides, for all he knew, these guys were law enforcement types.

"Take cover when you can," he ordered Kat tersely as he darted out from behind a palm tree to follow the black-clad men chasing her.

He was maybe thirty feet behind the last assailant when he spied Kat's lithe form ahead, slender and dark, sprinting through the trees. She dodged bushes and tree trunks with incredible agility, and the armed men fell back slightly. But then the lead guy raised his pistol.

"Incoming fire," Jeff bit out frantically. He was too close to the hostiles to be talking on the radio, but he had no choice. If they heard him and turned to fire on him, so be it. Unfortunately, he was too far away to tackle the guy with the gun.

He expected Kat to dive for the ground, to reduce her target profile to practically nothing, maybe even for her to roll on her back and fire back at the shooter. But instead, she picked up speed and literally ran up the trunk of a tree, momentarily going horizontal about six feet off the ground. She sling-shotted back down to the ground with an extra dose of momentum, zipped across the shooter's field of fire and took a running start at a medium-size palm tree. She ran the first eight feet or so up the trunk, then in one smooth move, slung a short rope around the tree, grabbed the free end as it whipped around the trunk, and used the rope and her feet to shimmy up the tree as fast as any chimp.

Jeff stared in disbelief. He'd never seen anything like it. Apparently, neither had the hostiles, for they both slowed to an incredulous jog, staring up into the treetops where she'd disappeared.

A moment later, a black shape hurtled out of a neighboring palm tree, swinging down and out on a long frond, landing lightly in the path well ahead of her pursuers. Then Kat was off and running again, this time with enough of a head start to duck into the deep shadows and vanish from sight.

Belatedly, the men took off running again. They slowed and peered into the area where she'd disappeared, but after thirty seconds or so of fruitless searching, gave up and turned to run for the road, where their buddies were shouting. Sounded like the other team wanted these two to join them already.

Jeff was stunned. He'd seen enough cheesy martial arts movies in his youth to know Hollywood's images of ninjas, but he'd never dreamed that any of the spectacular feats portrayed on film might actually be real. Had he not just seen that with his own eyes, he'd never have believed it possible.

A vehicle roared away, its sound disappearing into the night. Sounded like the Ghost was making his getaway on a motorcycle.

Kat panted into his earpiece. "Who are these guys?"

"No idea. They're acting military. Say status," he bit out.

"A van just pulled up. The men are getting in. I'm taking the car."

Jeff swore and veered toward the main road. He was in time to see their compact sedan peel out from behind the shrubs where he'd hidden it and take off down the road at high speed. Across the street, the last black-clad man piled into an unmarked white van, and the vehicle gunned its engine. Its tires spit gravel, and the rear end fishtailed as it pulled out onto the road, accelerating hard.

"They're giving chase," he called. "White van. Rear license plate obscured. Blacked-out windshield. You shouldn't have trouble spotting it. It'll be the only thing on the road behind you doing a hundred miles per hour."

"Thanks," Kat retorted.

"What in the hell were you thinking, leaving by yourself?" he demanded over his radio as he took off running futilely down the road behind the fleeing vehicles. Christ. She was out there by herself now, caught between the Ghost and those commandos. *And he wasn't there to protect her.* A cold fist of dread closed around his throat.

"I was thinking about not losing the Ghost," she replied tartly. "I'll let you know where he leads me. I just passed a moped rental place. It's about a quarter mile from the mansion. Hot-wire one if you can't wake up the owner. I might need backup."

"Ya think?" he snapped.

He cursed her roundly as he ran for all he was worth. His mind churned as fast as his legs. Who were those guys? He'd lay odds they weren't cops. D'Abeau knew they were staking out Shangri-La. The detective's men wouldn't have pulled weapons on him and Kat. Private mercenaries, then? Maybe hired by the homeowner to protect his art? But then why had they given chase to the Ghost and not stuck with the art collection? What private citizen bothered to or could afford to hire a half-dozen hard-core mercenaries, anyway? Such men did not come cheap.

Who, then?

They'd moved in when the Ghost came out of the house. Enemies of the thief's, perhaps? What did an art thief do to merit such enemies? Had he robbed the wrong man? Maybe stolen something besides art in a former job?

All that came into his mind were questions and more questions. He wanted some answers, dammit! He humped the quarter mile to the moped stand in about a minute. Not long in the real world, but a lifetime when his team was split up and an op was going to hell fast. After determining that the owner didn't live there, it took him another minute to break a flimsy chain lock on one of the mopeds and hot-wire it. A two-and-a-half minute head start for the

Ghost, Kat and the mystery commandos. More than a lifetime. An eternity.

Swearing under his breath, he peeled out of the stand and threw the throttle wide open. The lights of Bridgetown twinkled in the distance and a salt breeze whipped in his face, making his eyes water. He kept his mouth shut to avoid swallowing bugs and confined his cursing to silent epithets in his head.

Far ahead, a line of flashing sirens came into sight, racing down the highway toward him.

"He just turned off the main road," Kat announced. "Avoiding those cops, no doubt. Turn right after a supermarket sign—green letters on a white background. I didn't catch the name." Exertion strained her voice, and squealing tire sounds came over the radio along with her voice.

"Don't kill yourself chasing the bastard," he cautioned, his heart in his throat.

"Are you kidding? Offensive driving is a blast. I'd love to do this in the middle of a bunch of New York City cabbies sometime—show them what combat driving really looks like."

Jeff couldn't help grinning. She did sound like she was having fun. "Did the van make the turn behind you?"

A pause. "Looks like it. I see a cloud of dust behind me."

Kat continued to call out turns and mileages over the next several minutes, and he actually started to close the gap between them. Urban driving was as much about maneuverability as it was speed, and his Vespa was extremely nimble.

He spied a pair of taillights partially obscured by dust ahead and yelled into his radio, "I'm approaching the van. Where are you?"

"Just coming into Bridgetown proper. He's heading straight through the city. He knows we're back here. This could get ugly."

He snorted. Like it wasn't already? Would those men assume Kat was the Ghost's accomplice and take her out, too? He dared not risk it, no matter how bad he wanted to bag the Ghost. "Pull off the chase, Cobra. Lose the van. Make sure it's following the Ghost and leaves off you."

"This may be our only chance to catch the thief! I'm not stopping now. This island isn't that big. We'll corner him."

"And the guys behind you may kill you both. If you get in their way, they may very well shoot through you to get to him."

"I have been known to shoot back, you know. I'm not defenseless."

"One-on-six, you are."

She retorted rather sharply. "I'm a Medusa, not some average infantry grunt."

He swung wide around a corner, keeping his speed up and drawing a few more yards closer to the van. He supposed she was right. If she were a SEAL or a Ranger, he'd be a lot less worried about that van full of gunmen. She deserved the same benefit of the doubt as her male counterparts. At least that was what his head said. His heart screamed in denial. She was small and weak and female and he wanted her for his own. It was his job to protect her and keep her safe from jerks with guns.

"I stand corrected, Madam Medusa," he replied reluctantly.

"Watch the left turn in front of the school—you should hit it soon. It's a greater-than-ninety-degree turn and the road slopes away from you. Take it slower than it looks like you ought to."

"Roger."

The word was no sooner out of his mouth than the sound of screeching tires made him look up sharply. The van's grip on the road gave way as it careened around the very turn she'd just described. It teetered on two wheels and looked like it was going to settle back down onto all four when the right front fender clipped a parked car.

The van went airborne, sailing in a slow motion half roll a good thirty feet through the air. Then the front end hit the ground and the entire van snapped into a fast log roll, flying down the street sideways, flipping no less than six complete revolutions. Debris spun off in every direction. Jeff braked hard, dodging pieces of flying metal, swerving violently in and out among the litter. And then he was past the van.

He looked back over his shoulder and saw a man crawling out through the passenger's side window. As Jeff opened the throttle once more, he glimpsed the guy in his rearview mirror, limping over to the nearest parked car and smashing the butt of a rifle through the car's window. Those guys weren't done for yet. Whoever had survived the crash was going to hot-wire a car and come after them.

"The van crashed. But they'll procure another car and give chase. Where are you now?"

"Going into a residential area. A slum, actually."

"Keep calling your turns."

"Roger," she replied.

"How close are you to him?"

"I'm practically riding the back of his bike. A hundred yards, max."

She sounded distracted.

"He just took a right. First street past a crab shack. Red crab legs painted around a name on a white sign. Begins with a W or an M. Sorry I didn't see more."

He was amazed she was catching the details she was, what with driving like a bat out of hell, the darkness, and the adrenaline of the chase.

As the neighborhood deteriorated around him, Jeff cursed under his breath. Barbados, for all its wealth, had a few pretty rough areas. He didn't know whether to fear for Kat or for the locals if she got into a scrape in this neck of the woods.

Either way, he emphatically didn't want her alone. "Can you slow down a little?"

"Not if you don't want me to lose this guy. And by the way, he's small in stature. Lean. I'd estimate five foot seven at most, maybe 140 pounds. Great balance. A hell of a motorcycle rider. Black clothes, black ski cap, black gloves. Lemme see if I can get close enough to see his face."

A pause followed.

"Left at Old Joe's General Store. Looks like a little neighborhood market." And then she announced, "Third right after that, maybe a hundred yards past the store. It's a dirt road. No landmarks or sign. Be careful, it's narrow."

Then she said, "He just looked back over his shoulder. Caucasian."

Even this much information was a major breakthrough for the investigation. But Jeff would rather bag the guy and be done with it.

And then the sound of a gunning engine behind Jeff made him lurch. And swear. Looked like he had the crazy commandos on his tail now. He risked a glance back. They were still well behind him, no more than a pair of headlights in the distance. For now. Bastards were no doubt following the giant rooster tail of dust he was throwing up. But there wasn't a damn thing he could do about it. At least there was grim relief in the fact that now they'd chase him and not her.

Jeff flew down the road, pushing sixty miles per hour, keeping an eye out for the turn ahead.

"He just went up a set of stairs on his bike. I'm going on foot."

"You can't catch him on foot!" Jeff exclaimed. "Go around."

"I can catch him if he doesn't have a back tire."

Oh, crap. "Shooting is not authorized, Kat! You're in a residential area! Chock full of civilians—"

She cut him off. "Too late. I just took his bike tire out. Our boy's on foot. I'm closing."

"Don't engage him. I repeat, don't engage!" Jeff shouted into his mike.

No answer. Damn, damn, damn!

He slowed to take the next turn, and that engine behind him got a whole lot louder all of a sudden. The gunmen were going to catch him fast at this rate.

There was the first turn. He screeched around the corner, skidding violently. He slammed a foot down on the pavement, saving himself from a nasty wipeout. He righted himself, and accelerated with a screech of tires. Old Joe's. Old Joe's. C'mon, c'mon.

There it was. He took the corner way faster than he ought to have. One street. Two streets. Brake. Skid wildly around the third corner… Up ahead he spied their car, parked at an angle across half the narrow street, its driver's side door open.

He pointed the moped up the steps beside the vehicle, banging up their bone-jarring length. He burst out into an alley. Looked left and right. There. In the distance. A familiar dark, running figure disappeared around a corner. He pointed the moped that way. His back tire was getting soft. Didn't like that flight of stairs, apparently. *Hold together just a few more seconds, baby.*

He turned the corner and looked around this new alley frantically. His heart dropped to his feet. Two figures ahead, up high, racing across a rooftop. Crap. The Ghost and Kat were climbing now. He didn't stand a chance of following them up there. He rode along below them, trying to hear them above the wounded sound of his moped. It was no good. The bike was getting too difficult to control. He ditched it and took off running.

"Talk to me." He panted into his mouthpiece.

"Heading north," she bit out. She sounded like she was exerting herself pretty hard.

He made the next turn to head north. He passed a couple of tough-looking locals smoking weed in a doorway, but he went by so fast they hardly had time to react.

"Damn, this guy's agile," Kat complained. "He's jumping gaps."

"Don't fall," Jeff retorted in alarm.

"Huh."

The alleys got darker and narrower and dingier. He dodged sleeping goats and startled the hell out of himself when he narrowly avoided drop-kicking a chicken, who proceeded to take extremely loud umbrage at being awoken.

All of a sudden, intuition washed over him, certainty as real as the dirt beneath his feet. *Kat was in trouble.* As the hen squawked behind him, Jeff put on a burst of speed.

"Where are you, darlin'?"

Nothing.

"Click if you're running silent."

He waited. And waited. Nothing. Dammit! Even if she'd gone to ground and was hiding, she should've been able to ease a hand up to her throat to give him a lousy click on the radio to let him know she was okay.

Purely following his gut now, he slowed to a walk. It was a bitch to control his breathing, but he forced himself to breathe light and quiet. He thought he heard a scuff ahead. He raced toward the sound, pausing in the shadow of a doorway and easing around the corner.

Aw, hell.

He spotted two grappling figures teetering on the edge of a rooftop.

He took off running for all he was worth. "Hey!" he shouted at the Ghost.

One of the figures glanced up, startled. And then…oh, God…the fighting pair overbalanced. And fell, plummeting toward the ground two stories below.

"Kat!" he shouted frantically.

Chapter 11

The Ghost lurched in her grip and it was just enough to throw off the razor's edge of balance they both wavered upon. Kat only had time to register dismay before the two of them launched into space. The ground rushed up from below. She twisted to take the impact on her left hip and shoulder. But then something massively heavy crushed her, and that was the last she remembered.

"Kat. Honey, wake up."

She vaguely heard the words. Vaguely registered frantic hands running quickly over her body. She managed a groan.

"Don't move," the worried voice instructed.

She exhaled, managing with great effort to form words. "Go get him."

"To hell with the Ghost," Jeff snapped. "Can you feel your feet? Move your fingers for me, sweetheart."

Obediently, she wiggled her fingers, although it hurt every bone in her body to move even that small amount. She took as deep a breath as her battered body would tolerate and released it slowly, exhaling the pain as Hidoshi had taught her, closing it off in a remote corner of her mind, far, far away.

"How many fingers am I holding up?"

She squinted up at Jeff. The poor guy looked about ready to puke. "Uh, three."

"We need to get out of here. Those commandos are still behind us somewhere."

Before she had time to be startled, he'd scooped her up in his arms and stood up. It was a patently annoying display of manly special operator strength that she could never hope to duplicate. Although, at the moment she was profoundly relieved simply to relax in his grasp and let him carry her. Her head was spinning like a top and her body announced in no uncertain terms that it had had enough.

"You okay?" he muttered.

"Uh-huh," she managed to mumble back.

"Okay if I run?"

"Maybe not."

"I'm afraid we need to, darlin'. If you're gonna get sick, lemme know and I'll set you down."

Reluctant humor tugged at the corners of her mouth. "I'll bet you say that to all the girls."

He grinned down at her. "I don't generally pick up puking-drunk women. I like them reasonably sober and alert in my bed."

"That's right. You go for all that sparkling conversation."

He laughed under his breath. "No. I just like them conscious and able to scream my name."

"Picky, picky."

He must've heard her fading, because he murmured, "Just rest. I've got you."

Normally, she'd rebel in no uncertain terms if some guy said that to her. She was beholden to no man, thank you very much, and she certainly didn't need to be patronized by one. But damn, it felt good to close her eyes and let Jeff carry her swiftly into the bowels of the neighborhood. Where he was going, she had no idea. But he seemed sure of himself. And why not? He was a far more experienced operator even than she was.

Had she really run this far? Or was it just that she felt so crappy now that it seemed to be taking forever to get back to the car?

"There's that damn chicken again," Jeff muttered balefully. "He's lucky you're hurt or I'd stop and make fryer parts out of him."

She smiled against Jeff's powerful chest. He smelled salty, but she detected a sour note of fear in his sweat, too. Had he been scared for her? He'd sounded mostly pissed off at her on the radio earlier. She hadn't meant to ditch him. It was just the only way not to lose the Ghost.

"I got a look at him," she murmured. "Not a good one, but a look. Thick, dark eyebrows. Narrow nose. Slight droop to the outer corners of his eyelids. Small mouth. Full lips."

"Could you pick him out of a lineup?"

She considered the question. "Probably. But he'll change his appearance if he doesn't leave the island."

"True."

Jeff strode on in silence for several minutes. And then all of a sudden he ducked into a dark doorway and let go of her feet so her body slid down his torso to the ground. He glided left to put himself between her and whatever threat he'd seen or heard.

She knew better than to ask what he'd seen. When he could tell her, he would. She felt the zen calm flow over him that operators were taught when they needed to hide. She mimicked the action, too groggy to know if she'd eliminated the intangible essence of her presence or not.

"Let's move out," he breathed over his shoulder. "Nice and slow. You stay behind me."

She gave one tap on his back to indicate that she understood and would comply. Assuming she didn't pass out, of course. How long they crept down dark alleys, paused before corners and ducked behind various forms of cover, she had no idea. But she did know she ached from head to foot and the adrenaline of the chase had long ago worn off, leaving her nauseous and exhausted.

These were the moments Hidoshi had prepared her for in all those grueling years of training. She called upon his legacy now, and upon the legacy of the Medusas that endured any pain for the sake of the team. It was purely mind over matter. As long as she was conscious to will her body to move, she would keep going, no matter how agonizing.

Finally, after an eternity, Jeff murmured, "Here we are."

"Is it safe to take our car?" she mumbled.

"No. That's why we're taking this one. The owner left the keys hanging from the sun visor. I'll return it tomorrow. But right now, I need to get you back to the hotel and get some painkillers in you."

How he knew she was hurting, she didn't bother to ask.

He asked quietly, "Can you climb in?"

Strangely enough, after all the running around she'd just done, the act of bending down to duck into the tiny Peugeot all but made her pass out.

"Allow me," Jeff murmured as he scooped her off her feet and placed her gently in the passenger's seat.

Maybe it was the blow to her head that she'd taken in the fall, or maybe it was just her accumulated delirium that prompted her to murmur, "You are one serious hunk, Jeff Steiger."

He scowled at her. "You picked a hell of a time to tell me that, woman. You're half conscious and bruised from head to foot, and I can't do a damn thing about what you just said."

She grinned lopsidedly at him. "I am a little loopy, aren't I?"

"Oh, yeah. Let's get you out of here." He leaned her seat

back for her and buckled the seat belt across her hips. She wasn't sure which one of them was more surprised by the faint sigh of pleasure that escaped her as his hand ran across her lower belly. Quickly he went around to the driver's side and started the engine.

"I've got to call D'Abeau," he announced as he eased away from the curb.

She closed her eyes as Jeff guided the car back toward their hotel, presumably watching their tail for any signs of the commandos. As he drove, he dug out his cell phone and dialed the detective. She'd bet D'Abeau was pretty ticked off right about now. The Ghost was making fools of them all with these repeated and successful robberies.

Jeff identified himself, and through the phone, she heard the agitated sounds of D'Abeau throwing a hissy fit.

Jeff replied calmly. "Yes, I know. The Shangri-La estate. A Turner landscape, yes? We were there. Saw the Ghost break in."

Even she heard D'Abeau squawk, *"And you let him get away?"* More shouting ensued.

Jeff managed to interrupt the tirade with, "Can't come in right now. My associate's...not feeling well. We'll come down tomorrow and make a statement, but in the meantime here's the quick and dirty update." He proceeded to give a brief summary of what they'd seen and how they'd chased the Ghost into east Bridgetown, leaving out all description of her circus high-wire act antics with the thief.

She reached up to feel for her throat mike. Gone. At one point in the fight, the Ghost had grabbed at her throat and ended up with a fistful of high-tech electronics instead. It had seemed to surprise him. Enough that it had given her an opening to slip his hold and force him to the edge of that roof.

The thought of how badly that fall could've turned out accentuated the nausea rising in her gut. She settled into a simple mantra. Don't throw up. Don't throw up. Don't...

Eventually, the interminable car ride ended and Jeff pulled up behind the hotel.

"Can you walk?" he murmured.

"I think so. It'll draw less attention if I do."

Jeff grinned. "Either that or you'll have to act drunk off your ass."

"Very funny. I don't drink. I'm allergic to alcohol."

"Man, I'm sorry to hear that. It's the surest and fastest way to get a woman into my bed—ply her with enough booze to drop her inhibitions and blur her vision."

Kat followed him into the service elevator and smiled up at him foggily. She reached a hand out and steadied herself against his chest as the enclosure lurched into motion. "You're plenty pretty, big guy. No need for the girls not to be able to see you."

"Glad to hear you think so," he murmured low. He added lightly, "Especially since you're gonna be looking at this mug for the next eighty years or so."

She started to shake her head, but stabbing pain traveled across her skull and down her neck. She settled for grousing. "You and your Cupid's Bolt. Thing is, I don't play by Cupid's rules. I play by Medusa's."

"I'm okay with that if she shoots arrows of true love at her followers."

Kat stepped out into the soft night light of their hallway and murmured, "I wouldn't know personally, but her track record with my teammates isn't half bad."

"Give it time, darlin'," he murmured, smiling. "Give it time."

By noon the next day when Kat woke up, Medusa had definitely tossed a whole bunch of arrows at her, and they'd lodged in every part of her body, radiating waves of pain. Carefully, Kat climbed out of bed and headed for the hottest shower the hotel could offer up. She stood under the steaming jets until her muscles unwound a little and the pain had subsided from excruciating to merely miserable.

She took stock of her injuries. She had a spectacular bruise on her left hip, and the one on her upper left arm wasn't far behind. Her neck hurt, and she was generally stiff and sore. Although she had a smashing headache, she'd didn't have the blurred vision and piercing pain of a concussion.

The Ghost was no doubt fine. She'd cushioned his landing to the extent that he'd walked away completely unfazed from that fall. After all, he'd fled the scene quickly enough that Jeff hadn't been able to give chase. Or maybe Jeff had chosen not to give chase. Hmm.

She dressed carefully and made her way out to the spread of fresh fruits and pastries Jeff had obviously ordered earlier.

"How're you feeling?" he asked with concern.

"I'll live."

"That was a spectacular fall you took. I'm amazed you walked away from it."

She glanced up at him over the rim of her coffee cup. "I was pretty out of it, but the way I remember it, I didn't walk away from it."

Jeff shrugged as if slightly embarrassed.

"Not used to carrying your teammates home, huh?" she asked lightly.

That put a smile on his face. "Not unless they're pretty drunk, no."

She gave voice to her curiosity. "Why didn't you go after the Ghost?"

"You were down. No way was I leaving you if you were seriously injured. That was a rough part of town, and there was no telling whether or not anyone would've come out to help you. Besides, I couldn't take a chance on those commandos finding you while I was off chasing the Ghost. Our thief can wait. We'll get him next time."

"I can't imagine there'll be a next time," she retorted. "Surely, he'll jump the first plane out of here."

Jeff shrugged. "I dunno. D'Abeau and his boys have the

airport locked down tight. Your description is enough for them to work with."

She shook her head and immediately regretted the move. "He'll change his appearance radically. They won't recognize him if he decides to leave."

Jeff sighed. "You're probably right."

"Now what? How aggressively does General Wittenauer want us to pursue this guy?"

Jeff frowned. "We'll stay on it a little while longer before we give up and go home. At a minimum, we can keep an eye on the other pieces in that catalog. If one of them turns up missing, we'll know (a) that Viper's theory on the collector wanting the paintings in that catalog is right, and (b) we'll know the Ghost has *cojones* the size of an elephant's and is still here in Barbados."

"I'm sorry I lost him."

He stared at her in shock. "You nearly died trying to catch him. You went above and beyond the call of duty."

"But I failed."

"You can't win 'em all, Kat."

She flashed him a wry smile. "But that doesn't mean I can't try."

He laughed at that. "Spoken like a true Special Forces operative."

She fiddled with a croissant, shredding it into flaky pieces on her plate. "We may have a small problem."

"What's that?"

"Not only did I get a good look at the Ghost, but he got a good look at me, too."

Jeff asked quickly, "Did he threaten you while the two of you were grappling?"

"No. He didn't speak at all."

"Did he pull a weapon on you? A knife or a gun? Brass knuckles?"

"Nope. He fought me bare-handed."

"Sounds like an old-school art thief."

She frowned. "And that's significant why?"

"Used to be that art thieves weren't violent criminals. They didn't injure anyone in taking their prizes. In turn, the police usually didn't shoot them. They might end up in jail for fifteen or twenty years, but they didn't end up dead or sentenced to life in prison."

"And now?"

He shrugged. "Times have changed. Art thieves won't hesitate to kill guards or bystanders nowadays. But if this guy's old school, I doubt he'll come after you for knowing what he looks like."

"Gee. That's reassuring."

Jeff grinned at her across the table. "Hey. I've got your back. Nobody's killing you on my watch."

She smiled back at him. She knew it already, but it was nice to hear him say it. In fact, it made her feel a little embarrassed all of a sudden. Which was ridiculous. All special operators looked out for their teammates as a matter of course. It went without saying that he had her back and that she had his. Must be the blow to the head making her go all sappy and sentimental this morning. It couldn't have a thing to do with the memory of his worried voice when he'd reached her, or his protective arms cradling her close as he'd picked her up, or his gentle consideration getting her back to the hotel.

Frustrated with her train of thought, she asked briskly, "What's on the agenda today?"

"We need to visit D'Abeau. I did promise him we'd come in and make statements. If we hang around for a few more days and the Ghost doesn't strike again, then we'll head back to the Bat Cave and wait for something more to turn up on the guy."

She made eye contact with him across the table. It clearly galled him to think of going home empty-handed. Their kind didn't suffer defeat easily or well. She smiled bravely at him. "Maybe we'll catch a lucky break."

"In the meantime, we get to spend a few days in a beautiful tropical resort on Uncle Sam's dime. Gotta love this job."

She'd spent plenty of ops in below-zero temperatures or sweltering heat, had gone for weeks without a proper bath, had crawled through slime and muck and manure and suffered about every form of misery possible for a human to experience in her work. This elegant hotel and her lethally attractive companion weren't half bad. Not half bad at all.

The interview—or thinly veiled interrogation, as it turned out to be—with D'Abeau took most of the day and was a royal pain. After four grueling hours of browbeating, only flashing the detective her massive bruises seemed to convince him that she and Jeff had not been the thieves themselves. Never mind that U.S. government officials had verified that Jeff worked for them and that she was who she claimed, also. In fact, General Wittenauer personally told D'Abeau he'd assigned Jeff to investigate the Ghost. Interestingly enough, D'Abeau never challenged her affiliation with Lloyd's. She'd have to thank Michael again the next time she saw him—hopefully at his wedding to her teammate, Aleesha, later this year.

The sun was low in the sky and Kat was tired, sore, hungry and cranky by the time she and Jeff were allowed to leave police headquarters.

Jeff grumbled. "You hungry?"

She replied, "Starved."

"Want some seafood?"

"Perfect." Heck, shoe leather and wilted lettuce sounded delicious right about now.

They veered into the first authentic-looking place they came to—a pub crammed with cricket memorabilia and advertising the "Best Fish and Chips in the Lesser Antilles."

They ordered two plates of the house specialty, which turned out to be excellent. They spoke little. Not only were they in public, there wasn't much to say about the afternoon's waste of time. They'd told the truth, stuck to their guns, and no matter how suspicious D'Abeau was, their story had held up.

Kat found herself examining every patron who walked into the bar, comparing facial features against her indistinct impressions from last night. No sign of the Ghost. Of course, if she were the guy, she'd be hiding under the darkest rock she could find and trying to figure out the fastest way off this island. Frankly, she expected he was long gone. Bankrolled by someone rich and shady as he was, surely the Ghost had access to private transportation. She grimly recalled the long row of swanky charter jets parked at Sir Grantley Adam Airport when they'd arrived.

After the meal, Jeff asked, "How about a walk on the beach—or are you too sore for that?"

"It would probably do me good to work out a few of the kinks."

And so it was they came to be down on the waterfront, reveling in the pristine white sand as the moon rose, casting a pearlescent glow across the serene ocean.

Jeff smiled at her. "Pretty romantic, huh?"

She quirked an eyebrow back at him. "Are you fishing for me to fling myself into your arms and kiss you senseless?"

He regarded her much more seriously than she'd expected. He answered slowly, "No, I don't think flinging will ever be your style. You're more subtle than that. More sophisticated. In public, at least. I confess, though, that I am hoping you like to cut loose in private."

"What if I'm the world's worst kisser and terrible in bed? It would surely suck to be saddled with me for eighty years then."

He chuckled and closed the distance between them, bringing him squarely into her personal space. "Most skills can be learned. At the end of the day, it's all about how you feel, anyway. If you really care for someone and try to express that, nothing you do in bed is wrong. But if you're worried about it, I stand ready to give you expert instruction."

"You're incorrigible." He was so close she could breathe in his intoxicating scent. Since when had sniffing some guy made her head spin like this? Maybe it was left over from the blow to her head last night. But somehow, she didn't think so.

He murmured, "I prefer to think of myself as single-minded."

"Obsessed?"

He leaned even closer. The broad silhouette of his shoulders blocked out most of the ocean behind him. "Focused."

"You are tempting," she murmured reluctantly.

"Go ahead. Try me. I dare you."

Chapter 12

Jeff held his breath as Kat gazed up at him. *C'mon, baby. Take the plunge. Let go of all that self-control for just a second.*

Moving tentatively, she reached across the yawning chasm that was the last few inches between them to lay her hands on his chest. Her fingertips settled against his shirt, every bit as subtle and evocative as he'd anticipated. His entire being contracted with need. A need for more of her touch upon him. For satin flesh sliding across his, silky hair falling around them, ruby lips sipping at him…

"You know," she murmured, "I think I ought to bed you just to get it out of the way. Then we can both stop wondering what it would be like."

Bright fireworks colored by equal parts anticipation and disbelief exploded in his brain. Had she really just said that? She didn't have to give *him* that invitation twice. He turned immediately to head back for their car and their hotel room. Or more precisely, his big, comfortable bed in their hotel room.

She said earnestly, "We need to focus on the Ghost. But I'm afraid that until we both scratch this itch, we'll be performing at less than optimal levels."

"Brilliant logic," he managed to mumble. How he held himself back from falling upon her and ravishing her right there, he didn't know. It was a close thing. No, he wanted his butterfly to come to him willingly and unfold freely beneath his touch.

She stopped and turned to face him. Rose up on tiptoe. Reached up and twined her fingers in the short hair at the back of his neck. He stared down into her dark, dark eyes, surprised as something akin to trepidation flickered through them.

"Don't you know how crazy I am for you?" he whispered. "There's nothing to fear from me."

And that seemed to do it. She tilted her chin up the last fraction of an inch and their lips met. Her mouth was luxuriously soft against his, and he inhaled appreciatively, tasting sweetness on her breath. Their kiss was languid, a warm and easy thing this time, the slow savoring of something rare and exquisite. Gradually, she pressed herself against him, bit by bit losing her inhibition. For him, it was torture. Talk about self-control! But he *had* to let her set the pace.

Her tongue traced his lips, then ventured beyond, shyly inviting him to deepen the kiss. Groaning in relief, he accepted. His tongue swirled around hers, stroking approvingly. Her hips surged against his, and he blinked down at her in surprise. Her eyes were closed, the look upon her face rapturous in the moonlight.

She was going to be one of a kind when they finally got naked together.

He slipped his hand beneath her shirt, running his fingertips lightly up her spine. She shivered beneath the caress, and her entire body undulated against his. His brain locked up on the spot.

"We've got to stop doing this in public," she mumbled against his lips.

"You'll have to pull the plug," he muttered back. "I can't do it."

"Me, neither."

Their smiles met and merged as they became more familiar with one another, found the best angles of approach and retreat, explored more freely with hands and lips and tongues.

While the surf rolled in rhythmically behind them, the moon smiled down on them approvingly and a warm breeze wrapped them in the beguiling romance of the islands. Soft sand beckoned them to stretch out upon its residual warmth and succumb to the allure of the night and the moment.

"We're in trouble," she sighed.

"Why? Seems to me like we're finally working things out the way they're supposed to be."

She laughed ruefully. "Allow me to rephrase. I'm in trouble."

He drew back far enough to look down at her, but not far enough to break the delicious contact of her lithe body against his. "How so?"

"You're distracting me from being who I am."

"What if I'm helping you discover who you really are?"

She stared up at him. "You think so?"

"I know so."

"I want to believe you."

"Why don't we go scratch that itch and then see what you think?"

She smiled widely. "Let me guess. In your mind that logic is flawless."

"And it's not in yours? Honey, I can smell the desire on you. I can taste it. Hell, your entire body's humming with it. Your control has been superhuman. And, frankly, so has mine. Now that we've proven we can resist this thing between us, don't you think it's time to see what happens when we give in to it?"

That made her laugh. "I give up. Your argument is impeccable."

Thank God. He wasted no time heading for the new car the folks at the H.O.T. Watch had arranged for that morning. The drive back to the hotel was quiet. Kat sat, lost in thought. Hopefully, she was pondering which sexy little thing she was coming to bed in. He was just grateful that the awful tension of waiting was about to be over.

They didn't have to act to race through the lobby of the hotel like a pair of impatient lovers. They tumbled into the elevator, falling into each other's arms before the doors had even finished sliding shut. Only the ding announcing their floor tore them apart, and they took off racing down the hall to their room. He unlocked the door and held it for her with an old-fashioned bow that made her laugh.

She stepped past him into the dark, and as the hall door opened fully, the white sheers billowed into the room on a soft breeze.

Kat dropped into a defensive crouch and spun right, away from the opening. What the hell? He didn't question her reaction, though. He spun low and left, scanning the living room urgently as his eyes sluggishly adjusted to the dark. She glided on silent feet toward her bedroom door, and he headed for his. What in the world was going on? The room looked deserted. Felt deserted. Not that gut feelings were always reliable. A seasoned operator could fade into the woodwork right in front of you. He proceeded with caution, operating on the assumption that there was an intruder until a thorough search proved otherwise.

A quick glance under the bed was clear. He flung the closet door open and pushed aside all his clothes. Nothing. That left only his bathroom. On the way past his backpack, he pulled out a pistol. Behind the door—clear. Shower— clear. Linen closet—too small to conceal a man, but cleared nonetheless. He'd just started to straighten to his full height when Kat called out sharply from her bedroom.

"In here!"

His heart leaped into his throat. Was she in trouble? The protective instincts of a lion roared through him, and by the time he reached her bedroom door, he was in full kill mode. Nobody was messing with his woman. He burst through the half-closed door, looking around wildly for a target to blow away.

"Easy, Rambo. It's just a note."

"A note?" His mind didn't initially make sense of the word, so frantic was he to make sure she was safe.

"Yes. You know. A piece of paper with words written on it that kids pass back and forth in school without getting caught."

"What note?"

She pointed at her bed.

He looked, and tucked partially beneath her pillow was an envelope. "Can I turn on the light?"

"I doubt we'll be able to read the note unless we do," she replied dryly.

Scowling, he hit the light switch. Bright light flooded the room, and he squinted in its glare.

Kat reached for the envelope and he bit out, "Don't touch it."

She looked up, surprised. "You want to treat this as an explosive device?"

"Let's assume the worst until we check it out."

She shrugged and moved to her closet. She pulled out a small nylon bag and unzipped it. "Stand back."

While he stepped back, using the doorframe to block him from direct line of sight of the envelope, she pulled out a handheld meter and passed it over the note.

She announced, "No electronic or magnetic emissions."

He nodded tersely.

She used a long pair of tweezers to lift the edge of the pillowcase away from the note and pointed a flashlight beneath the eiderdown pillow. "No visible wires," she called.

"Any fluid stains or visible powder?"

She took out a magnifying glass and shone her flashlight

on the envelope for extra illumination. After a minute's examination, she shook her head. "Nothing. I think it's just a note."

"Any writing on the envelope?"

"Nope. It's plain linen. Cream colored. The kind that might come with personalized stationery."

"Do you have gloves to pick it up with?"

She glanced over at him. "If this is from who I think it is, he won't have left any fingerprints on it."

Jeff stared at her for a blank moment and then his brain finally kicked into gear. The billowing curtains. An open window. And they hadn't left any open this morning. Only one person he knew of would enter a fifth-floor hotel room through the freaking window. He remarked, "Let's see what the Ghost has to say to us. This should be interesting."

Kat picked up the envelope gingerly and opened it. She unfolded a single piece of paper, and he moved to her side swiftly to read over her shoulder.

I must speak with you. I appeal to the same honor you displayed last night in not killing me. It is a matter of utmost importance. My word of honor—I mean you no harm. Welchman Hall Gully. Tomorrow. Midnight. By the old entrance to Harrison's Cave.

It wasn't signed.

She tipped the heavy envelope over and a single Polaroid picture fell out into her hand. It showed a loosely unrolled canvas, its edges frayed like a painting that had been cut out of its frame. The Turner landscape.

Kat frowned. "The Ghost wants to talk to me?"

"So it seems. How'd he find you?"

She shrugged. "He could've followed us back to the hotel last night. It wouldn't be too hard to find out which room a certain petite Asian woman and her male companion are saying in. Heck, he probably knows the names we registered under."

"Perhaps he's hoping to find a higher bidder for his prizes."

Kat shook her head. "I think not. He'd go straight to his contacts in the art world for that."

"Maybe you scared the hell out of him and he's looking to negotiate a surrender?"

Again, she shook her head. "He was confident as he jumped those roofs. He was sure of himself and his ability to defeat me until the last moment before we fell."

Stunned at what she was implying, Jeff asked, "Are you suggesting that he actually could have taken you in that fight if you two hadn't fallen?" He found the idea of anybody matching her martial skills hard to believe.

Kat shot him an offended look. "He didn't stand a chance against me. I was trying very hard not to kill him, and that's why it was taking me a while to put him down."

He gaped. "You mean you had a chance to take him out and you didn't do it?"

She drew herself up and replied defensively, "That's correct."

"And why not?"

She huffed. "He wasn't trying to kill me."

"This isn't the eighteenth century and your meeting wasn't with pistols at dawn! Gentlemen's rules don't apply to hand-to-hand combat between you and some criminal you've been ordered to catch. You're a soldier, for God's sake. You're paid to *win*, dammit."

She spoke with angry precision. "I have *never* done this job for the money. If I did, I'd be a private mercenary and make ten times what the U.S. government gives me."

"So you let our target go because it wouldn't have been sporting to use all your skills on him." It wasn't a question. It was an outraged statement of fact.

He could not believe her! He didn't even know what articles of the Uniform Code of Military Justice she'd just blasted to smithereens, but he had faith she'd broken a bunch of them. Great. And as her commanding officer, it fell to him to make the charges against her. How in hell was he going to destroy her career—and furthermore, her honor—and salvage anything at all between them?

"Why does he want to talk to me?" Kat repeated, interrupting his furious—and increasingly panicked—train of thought.

"How the hell do I know?" he snapped.

"Focus, Jeff. I need your brainpower, here. We have to decide if I'm going to that gully or not."

"One thing I know for damn sure," he burst out, "you're not going to that meeting alone."

She sighed. "He wants to talk to me. If you come along, he may not show himself. He'd head for the hills and we'd never find out what's so bloody urgent that he went to all this trouble to contact us."

"You could be walking straight into a trap."

"So could he. Why would he expose himself like this to such danger? I kept up with him across those rooftops last night, and he fought with me. He has to know that I stand a real chance of taking him down if he and I go head-to-head."

"Maybe that's why he wants to meet you. He's reveling in the thrill of finally coming up against a challenge."

"I don't think so. He'd have taken more risks in his robberies to date if he was looking for a cheap thrill."

Jeff exhaled hard. She was right. At the moment, Kat was thinking a lot more clearly than he was.

He stated forcefully, "You need backup. No way am I letting you go to that meeting alone."

"Then we've decided that I am going?" she asked with infuriating calm.

"Oh, you're going, all right. But on my terms. Not the Ghost's."

Chapter 13

The next morning, Kat had just finished a grueling workout, punching, kicking, spinning and leaping her way through a difficult practice sequence, when a knock on the hallway door startled her. Jeff was not up yet, or at least he hadn't emerged from his room where he'd retreated angrily—and alone—last night.

Hard to tell what he was madder about—the fact that she hadn't killed the Ghost or that fact that she was determined to go to this meeting without him. It sure had blown the mood between them last night. And she'd *so* been looking forward to making love with him. An urge to throw a petulant tantrum stunned her. She never threw tantrums, let alone pouted. And she was on the verge of doing both.

She toweled off the worst of the sweat streaming down her face and cracked open the hallway door. She gasped in surprise and threw the portal wide open. "What are *you* doing here?" she exclaimed as four of her teammates piled into the suite.

Aleesha Gautier, temporary commander of the Medusas while Major Vanessa "Viper" Blake was on maternity leave, laughed richly. In the thick Jamaican accent she affected when she was stressed or amused, she replied, "Ahh, girly. De way me hears it, our little Cobra got herself a big ol' mon-fish on de hook."

Kat stared. "Where in the world did you hear that?"

"Why, from de fish hisself. He say to me, 'Git your happy self down here to de islands. Your sniper girlie need someone to watch her six.'"

Kat gaped. "Jeff called you?"

Aleesha nodded. "Dat he did."

"When?"

Misty, the team's resident gorgeous blonde, replied. "Last night. He said you're insisting on—I believe his exact words were—being a damn fool and not letting him back you up. He said you needed us."

Kat didn't know what to say. She was elated to have her teammates here to help. But she was shocked that Jeff had called them. Why not call in his own team, whom he was accustomed to working with and knew like the back of his hand? The answer was obvious, of course. Because she knew the Medusas like the back of her hand. Apparently, he'd deemed it more important for her to feel safe and in her comfort zone than for him to feel that way. The generosity of the gesture stole her breath away.

Karen Turner, the team's Amazon look-alike Marine, glanced around the suite. "So where is the good captain? The way we hear it, he's quite an eyeful."

"Who told you that?" Kat demanded.

Dark-haired Isabella Torres laughed gaily. "Captain Steiger was on Dex's team until Maverick was given his own team to command. Dex says he's quite the ladies' man." Dexter Thorpe was Isabella's significant other and a Special Forces operator, himself.

Embarrassed at this third degree about her love life, Kat asked Isabella by way of blatant distraction, "So, when is Dex going to make an honest woman out of you, anyway?"

Isabella sighed. "His father's trying to coerce him into taking over the family business again and Dex is frantically taking missions to stay out in the field and out of contact with his family. Which means we haven't had much chance to discuss that recently."

And given that Isabella's family wasn't too keen on her career either, Kat supposed Bella wasn't about to throw stones at Dex for hiding from his parents.

The door behind her opened and Kat turned swiftly. Jeff wore a pale blue polo shirt, white Bermuda shorts and deck shoes. He looked like a bronzed god. His hair was neatly combed, still damp from his shower, and his eyes glowed bright blue, so sexy her knees went weak just to look at them.

He flashed a cover-model smile and drawled in his irresistible Southern accent. "You must be the Medusas I've heard so much about. It's a pleasure to meet y'all."

Misty muttered under her breath, "Way to go, Cobra!"

The other women grinned appreciatively as Aleesha held out her hand. "I'm Aleesha Gautier. Or you can call me Mamba. I'm nominally in charge of this gaggle."

Jeff stared at her hand cautiously, then spared a quick glance over at Kat. "She's not going to do the same thing you did the first time you shook my hand, is she?"

Kat did something she rarely did. She blushed to the roots of her hair. "Not unless you call her baby, too."

The other women's eyebrows shot up en masse, and unholy amusement glinted in their gazes. She'd forgotten how nothing was secret or sacred among them. Becoming a Medusa had come with inheriting five nosy, if well-meaning, sisters. If they caught wind of the depth of her infatuation with Jeff, they'd razz her until she wished she'd never met any of them.

Kat sighed and made introductions all around, including the snake field handles of all her teammates.

Aleesha asked briskly, "So. What's up?"

Kat sat back and let Jeff bring the team up to speed. He gave a good briefing. Quick. To the point, but thorough.

Aleesha said to him when he finished, "Since you're the expert on this case and have already been named mission commander, how 'bout you take point on this? Has Cobra briefed you on our various specialties?"

"No, ma'am. She hasn't said much about you ladies. But if she's any indication, you're a hell of a team."

More amused glances shot Kat's way.

Aleesha smiled broadly. "Call me ma'am again, boy-o, and I may 'ave to hurt you. You makin' me feel olduh dan dirt."

Jeff grinned back. "Duly noted, Mamba."

Aleesha gave him a quick rundown of who did what on the team. They all were cross-trained in a wide variety of skills, but Karen was the pro at things mechanical, Isabella was the team's intelligence analyst, Misty was a pilot and a whiz with computers and Aleesha was the team's medic. In fact, she'd been a trauma surgeon prior to becoming a Medusa.

Jeff looked faintly shell-shocked when Aleesha finished the recitation of the team's skill set. But he said calmly enough, "Have you ladies had breakfast?"

Karen laughed. "We're commandos. We're always hungry."

Kat made a room-service order for six while Jeff pulled out a detailed map of Barbados and showed the Medusas where tonight's meeting was supposed to take place.

The four other Medusas spent the afternoon casing Welchman Hall Gully, a gorgeous park/walking trail tucked into one of the many gullies slashing across the island's landscape. Kat retreated to her room to meditate until they returned, and Jeff left after mumbling something about getting some special gear for tonight.

It was just as well they stayed apart. Her teammates were

far too perceptive to miss the sparks—either of sexual tension or anger—that inevitably flew between them when they spent more than two minutes together. And Kat really could do without the Medusas' teasing.

Late in the afternoon, they all reconvened to finalize a plan of action. The caves beneath the gully were going to be a problem. They were extensive, and there was no way the Medusas could reconnoiter, let alone cover, all of them tonight. If the Ghost wanted to emerge from or escape into the caves, they'd be hard put to intercept him. The team settled on forming a loose net around Kat and planning to let the Ghost slip into it unmolested.

"And are you going to let him leave in peace as well?" Kat asked Jeff as they sat around the dining table, with maps and sodas scattered across it.

He looked her square in the eye for the first time all day. "No, I am not."

"But—"

He cut her off. "Don't argue with me on this, Kat."

"I am going to argue with you on this. There's no way the Ghost would have set up this meeting unless he has something of the utmost importance to tell me. We owe him the courtesy of hearing him out and giving him free passage away from the meeting."

"We owe him nothing. He's a criminal."

"He could've tried to kill me last night. But he didn't."

"You could've killed him, too, but you didn't. I'd say you two are even on that score."

Kat flinched as her teammates stared at her.

Aleesha asked quietly, "Cobra? Are you okay?"

"Yes," she grated. "I'm fine. Jeff seems to think that honor counts for nothing, however. And he's prepared to trample mine."

Aleesha looked over at Jeff soberly. "Mon, de girl, she take dat honor wicked serious."

He exhaled heavily. "Yeah. I know." He paused. "Our orders are to stop the Ghost. Using whatever means necessary. Nothing in our orders precludes use of force. As mission commander, I have to assume that implicit in our mission orders is not only permission to use force but a directive to do so if it will accomplish the mission."

Kat winced. Jeff had resorted to legalese for one reason and one reason only. He was warning her that he'd given her a lawful order—to use force if necessary to apprehend the Ghost. And furthermore, if she failed to do so, he'd hold her liable for having disobeyed a direct order.

Sure enough, on cue he said grimly, "Do you understand me, Captain Kim?"

"Yes, and I acknowledge that you have given me a lawful order. Do you want that in writing?"

She looked up from her tightly clenched hands at him across the table. His stare gave away nothing. No pity, no compassion, no caring. Just the hard, cold gaze of a military commander putting a subordinate sharply and unquestionably in her place.

So. That was how it was going to be.

Anguish wrenched her heart messily in two as she sat there, frozen, her face totally devoid of expression. Damn Hidoshi for teaching her this terrible control, anyway. She wanted to scream and cry and rage, to argue with Jeff about the stupidity of his decision, to demand to know how he could cut her off like this. Worse, she desperately wanted to beg him to look at her the way he had last night in the moonlight. To love her a little. But here she sat, as cold and lifeless as some plastic mannequin who didn't feel a damn thing.

Jeff sighed heavily and looked away from her.

Meanwhile, her teammates stared back and forth between the two of them in nothing less than open shock. As well they should. She'd never shown a single hint of temper, let alone defiance, in all the time any of them had known her.

Damn. Damn, damn, damn.

She'd known from the very beginning that it would never work between her and Jeff. And sure enough, it had come to this.

She stood up from the table and said woodenly, "I'm going for a walk. I'll be back in time for the final briefing."

Kat was mildly surprised that none of the Medusas followed her down to the beach. But she supposed they were so stunned by her outburst that they didn't know what to do. She'd been walking aimlessly along the beach for about an hour, oblivious to the magnificent sunset glinting scarlet off the pristine sand, when her cell phone rang.

Reluctantly, she pulled it out. Startled at the caller, she opened the phone. "Hi, Vanessa. Did the others sic you on me?"

"Hi. And yes, they did. Wanna talk?"

"If I say no and hang up, will you call me back continuously until I do talk to you?"

"No. I'll be on the first plane down there to get in your face until you talk to me."

Kat sighed. The woman would do it, too. Vanessa wasn't known for taking no for an answer. Thing was, of all her teammates, her boss came the closest to understanding her. She sometimes thought Vanessa had an inkling of her true capabilities but chose to honor her secret. Vanessa also seemed to have a handle on Kat's view of things like honor and right and wrong.

Kat asked in resignation, "What did they tell you?"

"That Captain Steiger, while making a rational mission decision, is forcing you into doing something he shouldn't."

Her teammates had supported her? She ought to have expected it, but it surprised and pleased her nonetheless. "They said that?"

"Aleesha said he asked you to go against your personal code of honor. She's worried that you'll disobey him and get in trouble."

Kat didn't reply.

"Will you disobey him?" her boss pressed.

"No offense, Vanessa, but I'll face a court-martial rather than go against my code of honor. I know you'll think I'm a fool, and you can tell me how I'm throwing away my career, but it's who I am. I can't go against my prom—" she broke off, horrified at what she'd just revealed.

"I don't think you're a fool, Kat. And I'd never ask you to go against the vows you made to your grandfather."

Kat practically dropped her phone. "How do you know about him?"

Vanessa had the good grace to sound apologetic. "I talked to Captain Steiger a few minutes ago."

Kat's stomach burst into butterflies. Not the excited, happy kind. The nervous, unpleasant ones. When Vanessa didn't continue, she asked reluctantly, "What did he say?"

"He loves you, Kat."

"He *said* that?"

Vanessa laughed. "Are you kidding? Of course he didn't say it. He probably doesn't even know it himself yet. But he's a wreck. He's tearing himself in two over what he believes to be his duty and his feelings for you. He could hardly form a coherent sentence when he was talking to me. He's a mess."

"Then how do you know how he feels?" Kat challenged.

"Because I watched Jack go through the exact same thing."

Jack Scatalone. Their training officer and supervisor, and Vanessa's husband. The man who'd been assigned to train the Medusas—and to break them. He'd been ordered to make sure they never became Special Forces operators. Except no matter what he'd thrown at them, they'd survived and succeeded. He'd reluctantly come to the conclusion that they deserved to take their place in the Spec Ops community, yet he'd been ordered to dismantle the team regardless of his pleas to let the Medusas have a shot. And to top it off, he'd been falling in love with Vanessa at the same time he was forced to sabotage her team.

Of all people, he probably was the one who could best understand the dilemma Jeff found himself in. Vanessa probably got it, too. Heck, even Kat could understand why Jeff was doing what he was doing. But that didn't mean she could meekly go along with it.

"Look, Vanessa. The Ghost appealed to my honor. He gave me his word that he meant no harm and that this meeting was vital. If I show up, I'm tacitly giving him my word in return that I won't pull any stunts on him. I *can't* take the guy down."

"Any idea why this thief wants to talk to you so much?"

"We've been chewing on that all day. No one has any idea. We all agree it's insane, and something compelling must be driving him to it."

"Does he know who you are?"

Kat mulled that one over. "He probably has a good idea. He ripped off my throat mike during the fight. When I hit the ground, it was gone, so he must've taken it with him."

"And after examining it, he'd probably have a pretty good idea that he's dealing with at least a U.S. government agent, if not a military member. Not too many civilians have access to the caliber of equipment we use. Let's assume he does know roughly who you are."

Kat frowned. Okay. So that only made his request to meet her all the more puzzling. Vanessa was quiet on the other end of the phone, and Kat didn't fill in the silence. Viper's intellect was formidable, and her instincts were pretty much without exception spot-on.

Finally, Vanessa sighed. "Jeff said this guy was old school. Carried no gun and made no effort to do serious injury to the two of you. Is that your impression of this guy as well?"

"It is."

"Something extraordinary has happened. Something he wants the American government to know about—badly enough to risk his life to tell it to you. You're the logical person for him to approach. Particularly since you could've killed him and didn't. You've earned a measure of trust from him."

Kat burst out, "And Jeff's asking me to betray that trust!"

"I'll talk to Jeff. You go to that meeting. Do what you have to do."

"Are you telling me to follow Jeff's order?" Kat asked in disbelief.

"I'm telling you to follow your heart. You've got more courage and decency in your pinkie finger than most people muster in a lifetime. I'm telling you to do what you think is right. Then, no matter what consequences follow, I'll back you up and you'll be at peace with yourself."

It was as if a wash of cool water flowed over her, flushing away all the bad energy, all the anger and disquiet making her sick at heart. Kat took a deep breath. Released it slowly.

"Thank you, Vanessa."

"There's nothing to thank me for. I told you to do what you were already going to do anyway."

"I haven't made up my mind—"

"Sure you have."

"Huh?"

"You're the heart and soul of my team. The arrow on the Medusas' compass that always points us in the right direction. You never waver; you always know the right thing to do. Whenever I'm not sure of what I'm doing, I can always look into your eyes and see exactly what I'm supposed to do. Tonight, I hear in your voice that you know the right thing to do. And I'm telling you to go with it. You've never steered me wrong before. I've no reason to believe you've read this one wrong, either."

Kat was speechless. Such a ringing vote of confidence from Vanessa, whom she arguably admired more than any other person alive, was overwhelming.

"You still there, Cobra?"

"Uh, yeah. Thanks. Wow."

Vanessa laughed. "So does this mean Junior and I get to stay home to look after my swollen ankles and eat chocolate tonight?"

Kat chuckled. "You do realize you've probably just signed the death warrant on my career, don't you?"

"You know, about half the folks in the Spec Ops community said Jack would never make colonel because he broke every rule in the book to bring the Medusas into existence. The other half said he was a shoo-in for colonel precisely because he broke every rule in the book and brought the Medusas into existence. And here he is, sporting a shiny new set of eagles on his shoulders. Risk takers are rewarded more often than not, Cobra. You'll come out of this okay."

"I'll hold you to that."

"I'll stand beside you no matter what happens."

Too bad Jeff couldn't say the same thing. "Thanks, boss."

"Any time."

In a much calmer frame of mind, Kat performed an ancient tai chi routine as the sun slid away into the west. She had a job to do, Jeff or no Jeff. And she would not fail Vanessa or the Ghost. She would live up to both of their best opinions of her.

No matter what Jeff did to her for it.

Chapter 14

Thankfully, the last-minute preparations for the meeting kept Kat—and Jeff—occupied enough that she didn't have to speak to him alone before they left for the rendezvous.

As soon as they arrived at the park, Jeff and her teammates melted away into the sultry stillness at the bottom of the sheltered valley. She was left to cool her jets in the car and listen to the others murmur over the radio as they covertly searched the park and moved into position to observe the meeting. The Medusas found no sign of the black-clad men from last night's robbery.

And then the waiting began.

Typically, when Kat waited before a kill, she dropped into a state of relaxation where time flowed over her and around her without touching her. But tonight she was unable to achieve that fugue state of waking sleep. She fought back jitters over and over. Under normal circumstances, if she were this agitated, she'd step away from the shot and let someone else take it. But tonight there was no one else. The Ghost would speak to her and her alone.

Finally, eleven-forty-five flashed on her watch. She got out of the car gratefully and made her way into the deserted park. Jeff had decided she'd move into place early to give the team of assailants from the last robbery plenty of time to reveal themselves.

She went to the bench and sat down. Acutely aware of the eyes of her team upon her, she schooled herself to utter stillness. After all, she had a reputation to maintain. The Medusas often called her the ice cube when she was waiting to make a kill. She could sit for two or three days with barely a twitch. She could surely sit on this bench for ten minutes without fidgeting.

But it turned out to be surprisingly hard to do. She was used to being the hunter, not the hunted. She knew all too well how easy a target she was, motionless and out in plain sight like this. Even the most inexperienced of snipers could pick her off like a tin duck in a cheap shooting gallery.

Must think about something else.

Jeff was out there. He'd never let anyone take a potshot at the future mother of his children—good Lord, had she just thought that? Since when had she bought in to his crazy notion of love at first bolt?

Good thing the Medusas had shown up when they had, or she might have been in serious danger of doing something entirely inappropriate in the middle of a mission. Except why didn't she feel relief at that thought? Why was vague disappointment at her team's inconvenient timing rattling around in her gut instead?

Jeff would be looking at her right now. He'd assigned the Medusas to scan the forest while he watched the immediate vicinity around her. Was he undressing her with his eyes? Imagining what they could've done together last night had they not had their argument? Whatever was on his mind, the heat of his gaze was palpable at a distance of a hundred yards or more. Or maybe that heat was coming from her own risqué thoughts. There was no question in her mind that he'd be a skilled lover. He was too comfortable with women, too physical a being, too at home in his own skin to be anything else.

Midnight came and went.

And still she sat. Alone.

She'd expected this, however. The Ghost would approach carefully, reconnoiter the area. Make sure she hadn't set a trap for him. *Come in, already, Mr. Ghost. My friends won't hurt you. Not if I have anything to say about it.*

The bench she sat on faced the main walking path that wound through the gully. Behind her fell a curtain of hanging vines and ferns from a stone arch that had once supported the ceiling of an ancient cave. Beyond the vines, the eroded remains of several massive stalagmites marked what used to be the cave floor. Between them, a faint path led the way back to an old entrance to Harrison's Cave—an extensive complex of caves stretching away beneath her feet. An iron security gate blocked the cave entrance to protect the caves from the local kids and vice versa.

"Don't turn around."

The whispered voice was quiet, barely reaching her ears. Male. Strongly French accented.

"Are you alone?" he asked.

"Of course not. My partner wouldn't hear of me coming out here by myself. He's hiding in the trees somewhere."

Two things happened simultaneously. Jeff swore sharply over the radio into her earbuds as he realized she was speaking aloud—off radio, and a quiet laugh floated out of the darkness behind her.

"Such refreshing 'onesty. I like you."

"Why did you want to speak with me?"

"Yes, let us go directly to the point. The danger this night is much greater than your friend."

She asked quickly, "What are you talking about?"

"As you may know, I 'ave been busy 'ere in Barbados."

She answered dryly, "So I've heard."

Another chuckle. "When a fisherman casts 'is net, 'e hopes to catch one kind of fish. But often, 'e catches another as well. Like the fisherman, I took a painting, but by accident, I took something else as well. Something you need to see. It was affixed to the back of a canvas."

"What is it?"

"In a moment. First, you must tell me true. Do you work for the American government?"

"I do."

"Perfect. If you will come over to the gate behind you, I will give it to you."

Startled, she stood up. The movement caused a flurry of chatter in her earpiece as the Medusas readied themselves for her to go mobile. She picked her way with exaggerated caution toward the gate, both because it was dark and hard to see in the shadow of the thick curtain of vines, and also to give her teammates a few extra moments to reposition themselves.

Isabella was the first to announce that she'd acquired a heat signature inside the opening to Harrison's Cave.

Kat murmured low, "Step back from the opening a little. My colleague has you in his sights." She might be willing to save the Ghost's life tonight, but she wasn't foolish enough to give away to him the true degree of backup she had out here.

"Merci." The French voice took on a faint echo as he spoke from farther inside the cave.

"Do you want me to come in there?" she asked as she approached the heavily padlocked gate.

"It is not necessary. Please, if you will reach your hand through the bars…".

She did as the Ghost directed.

Something smooth and flat that felt like cardboard was laid in the palm of her hand. "What is this?"

"This—'ow you say—self-explanatory."

"A warning, my friend. This time we have met in honorable truce. But I cannot extend that to you after tonight. My boss has ordered me to use whatever force is necessary to stop you. And next time, I will be bound by that order."

"Understood. In return, I 'ave a warning for you as well. If anyone finds out that I 'ave given this disk to you, you will find yourself in immediate and extreme danger. Be very careful."

"Danger from whom?" she asked, startled.

"You spared my life—for we both know you could 'ave killed me if you wished—and now I 'ave paid you back. Equal warnings 'ave we traded as well. I count us even."

She drew her hand back through the gate, tilting the cardboard sleeve in her hand to pass it through the metal bars. It held a CD of some kind.

Jeff announced sharply, "H.O.T. Watch says we've got heat signatures incoming. Four hostiles. Moving fast. Armed."

Kat started. She'd momentarily forgotten that the folks in the Bat Cave were monitoring tonight's meeting via surveillance satellite. She murmured, "The men who chased you from the scene of last night's theft are coming. Time to go, my friend."

"What men?" The Ghost's question was sharp. Alarmed.

He didn't know? She thought fast. Should she warn him or not? Maybe they were some law enforcement agency that the H.O.T. Watch wasn't aware of working on the case. If she gave the thief any more information, she could be compromising a criminal investigation. Except she'd already revealed the men's existence. And her gut instinct said to tell the Ghost about the men.

Jeff spoke in her ear. "Move out, Kat. Take cover."

She spoke fast. "Last night. Six men. Armed. Wearing

black. White van. They staked out the estate. While I was chasing you, they were chasing both of us."

"What 'appened to them?"

"Their van crashed. We took measures not to be followed home. Do they know who you are?"

Jeff's voice was more urgent. "Get out of there, Kat! They're almost here. We don't need a firefight out here."

The Ghost murmured, "*Merci.* I am in your debt once more."

Kat felt his swift departure into the bowels of the cave as a faint whiff of air against her skin. She took a quick look around and dove behind the curtain of hanging vines. Lying on a bed of moss, she announced quietly over her throat mike, "He's gone."

Jeff snorted and muttered, "And they're here. Everyone pull back. Quietly. No confrontation."

Kat reached out with her senses, hearing, smelling, even tasting the verdant night around her. If she crawled on this tender moss, it would rip, leaving obvious black gashes to mark her passage. Moving slowly, she drew her pistol and held it over her head with both hands in a firing position. Then she began to roll, gradually easing away from the cave opening. With each revolution, her gaze roved all around, seeking any movement, any shadow that was not of the night and of the forest.

Without warning, a tall figure clothed in black rose up about thirty feet beyond her head. She froze, lying on her back, gazing awkwardly up and back at him as he swung up a semiautomatic carbine in a smooth motion. In an instant, she identified the weapon. A Yugoslavian SKS rifle with a bayonet mount. Not a weapon Jeff or the Medusas used. And the guy obviously had a target in sight. The weapon settled against his shoulder and his right forearm tensed. He was firing!

Without hesitating, she squeezed off two shots overhead

while lying on her back. The first shot caught him under the right ear. The second, she'd adjusted downward to compensate for his beginning to collapse, and it hit him square in the temple. A kill shot.

The guy dropped like a stone as crashing sounds erupted from all directions. Men shouted back and forth. They yelled in a language she didn't know, but she didn't need to understand. They knew they had a man down, that there was a shooter out here, and they were determined to find and kill her.

This scenario, she knew. The kill was always easy. The escape afterward was hell. She rolled fast across the remaining moss, then rose into a crouch behind a tree trunk. She glanced up. A towering black pine. Not ideal for climbing… the branches were too thin to support much weight, and closely spaced enough to make scaling the trunk a pain in the rear. But she didn't have much choice.

She often made use of three dimensions when egressing a close-range kill. Most people only thought in two dimensions, so thinking vertically gave her a big edge. Not to mention, Hidoshi had trained her to climb like a monkey.

Not worrying about noise as the dead man's colleagues crashed through the gully like a herd of bull elephants, she jumped for the nearest branch. The soft wood bent deeply beneath her weight, but held.

Up she went, distributing her weight as best as she could among multiple branches as she climbed the rough ladder of limbs quickly. A dark shadow moved below, and she froze, one arm around the trunk, the branch she stood on slowly flexing beneath her weight. As the angle of the limb grew steeper and steeper, she prayed silently.

Hold a few more seconds. Don't crack.

Thankfully, the sap-filled wood remained silent, and the shadow moved on. She switched quickly to another branch and wrapped both arms around the trunk, supporting most of her weight that way.

"Where the hell are you?" Jeff murmured.

"I went vertical. One hostile just passed beneath me," she breathed back.

Misty murmured, "I have one moving past me, away from the park entrance."

Isabella spoke next. "I have one examining the downed man."

Frustratingly, no one reported sighting the last man. Kat was startled when Jeff breathed, "Ops, say location of hostiles."

A new voice came up on their frequency. "Two hostiles, immobile, sixty feet east of Cobra. One moving northwest, one-hundred-ten feet north of Sidewinder. One hostile moving west-by-southwest, approximately fifty feet from Python's location."

Kat mapped the locations in her head. Nobody was about to stumble across her hiding spot.

The voice continued. "A new hostile moving between Adder and Mamba's positions. Field-of-fire conflict between Adder and Mamba. Maverick, another tango is heading toward you. Should pass twenty to twenty-five feet in front of you, moving left to right. If you have cover and hold position, you should be clear."

Six men were out here? Those last two might have successfully ambushed the Medusas had the H.O.T. Watch combat observers not warned them. Handy, having an infrared picture from God's-eye view like this.

Jennifer Blackfoot came up on frequency. "Visual shows one more hostile back in the parking lot. He appears to be tampering with your vehicle."

Kat's jaw dropped. Okay, so the H.O.T. Watch folks were more than handy. They were lifesavers.

"Copy," Jeff murmured. "I have my man in sight."

The woods and the radios went silent as the hostiles calmed down from their initial panic and went into hard-core hunting mode, creeping stealthily through the lush tropical foliage.

It was a deadly game of cat and mouse. For the most part, Kat, Jeff and the Medusas held their positions, hunkered down to wait out the hostiles as the H.O.T. Watch observers occasionally murmured a position update.

And then Jennifer announced, "Problem, folks. We just got a momentary visual on one of your hostiles. We enhanced the image, and he appears to be wearing night-vision goggles. We cannot confirm, but have to assume they're infrared."

Kat's stomach dropped. That meant they also had to assume that their trackers could see them now, and would shoot them on sight. The rules of this game had just changed completely.

Jeff breathed into the radio. "Request permission to go full offensive."

Chapter 15

Kat held her breath while a long pause ensued. Then Jennifer spoke crisply. "Pull out of there. Attempt not to kill them, but shoot your way out of there as necessary."

Jeff murmured, "Copy. Medusas, rendezvous at Point Alpha."

The Medusas always established several rendezvous points in case they got separated on an op.

Jennifer spoke again. "Cobra, if possible, please confirm your kill and search the body. Who are those guys?"

Kat shimmied down out of the tree quickly, her gloves and shoes sticky with sap. She raced for the man she'd shot. She stared when she got to his body. His pockets were already turned inside out, his left wrist flung wide—and minus a watch. His weapon was gone. He wore no ammunition belt, and she thought she remembered glimpsing the bulge of one when she'd taken the shot. But she'd been firing from a wacky angle. Maybe she was wrong.

"This guy's been stripped of all identification," she reported.

Jeff ordered, "Converge on me, ladies. Ops, if you'd vector them in?"

The H.O.T. Watch controllers obliged, and Kat followed their directions toward her teammates. She thought hard as she ran lightly through the trees. Her kill's identity had been sanitized by one of his buddies. Which was pretty sophisticated behavior for common thugs. These guys were pros.

Jennifer Blackfoot came back up. "We just picked up a phone call to the Bajan police. Gunshots were reported. Time to leave the area. ETA on police—five minutes."

Dang. The H.O.T. Watch had the capacity to monitor local phone calls, too?

Jeff started, "Raven, about our vehicles. The cops—"

Jennifer cut him off. "Carter's calling the police now to tip them off anonymously that the cars may be rigged to blow up."

"Thanks," Jeff replied.

Kat was close to their rendezvous point and reached it in about a minute. She topped a steep outcropping of rock and spotted a crouching figure before her. A hand signal flashed. *Jeff.* She flashed back an all's well and he waved her in. She moved to his side while they waited for the others to join them.

"You okay?" he asked quietly, off radio.

She was startled to realize that the very same question had been on the tip of her tongue to ask him. Thing was, she already knew he was uninjured. And yet, she felt a need for reassurance. Her hands wanted to run over his limbs and torso and face, to check for injuries. Weird. She answered, likewise off radio, "I'm fine. You?"

"Fine. Why'd you shoot that guy?"

It did not escape her that he was giving her the benefit of the doubt—that he was assuming she'd had a good reason to disobey his order not to shoot and giving her a chance to share it with him. "The tango stood up, took aim, and started to fire at one of you." She shrugged. "There was no time to ask for a modification of your order."

He nodded briskly. "Okay. You'll need to write it up, of course."

She nodded, profoundly relieved. No questions. No second-guessing. He believed her story. Trusted her judgment. The paperwork of making an unauthorized kill was routine.

Karen and Isabella popped over the ridge next, and as sirens became audible in the distance, Aleesha and Misty joined them.

Jeff looked around. "Who's your pacesetter?"

The slowest runner always set the pace, and the others stayed with her.

Aleesha answered. "Me or Isabella, depending on who's carrying the most weight."

Isabella grinned. "Hey, I've been working out like crazy."

Aleesha grinned back. "I'm it, then. Let's go."

Kat fell in behind Python in the Medusas' usual retreat order. Not surprisingly, Jeff assigned himself to bring up the rear—the most dangerous position in a fighting retreat. They ran steadily until they emerged from the park. Aleesha found a narrow road, and took off down it.

They ran hard for nearly an hour before the lights and noise of a village came into sight ahead of them. Jeff called a halt. They pulled off the road into a clump of tall weeds. He pulled out a map and spread it out on the ground between them. "I place us here. Do y'all concur?"

Kat glanced at the map and nodded her agreement.

Jeff continued. "It's too far to run to any major town from here tonight. We can either obtain wheels or find someplace to camp."

Kat spoke up. "I vote for wheels. I want to see what the Ghost gave me and we'll need a computer to do that."

Jeff stared at her. "He gave you something?"

"Looks like a computer disk. He said he found it by accident. It's why he wanted to meet me."

Jeff nodded. "Wheels it is, then. Who's good at hot-wiring cars?"

Aleesha laughed. "Boy-o, we be de Medusas… Lay dem baby blues on how we do business."

Misty stood up, grinning. "Kat, your shirt, please. Maverick, if you wouldn't mind turning your back…"

Kat stripped out of her close-fitting black turtleneck while Misty did the same. They quickly traded shirts. Additionally, Misty popped off her bra before pulling Kat's shirt over her head. The effect never failed to startle Kat. The black fabric was skintight and left shockingly little to the imagination.

Misty announced, "You can turn around now, Maverick."

He did so. Kat didn't blame him for gulping. Misty was magnificently endowed, and Kat's three-sizes-too-small shirt showed the girls off to full effect.

"Well, then," Jeff commented dryly. "That's certainly…informative."

Kat's eyes twinkled as he glanced over at her, clearly checking to make sure she wasn't jealous of his reaction to Misty's display.

"Pass me your cash, ladies," Misty muttered as she applied mascara, using a small mirror Karen lit for her with a flashlight.

While Misty finished putting on eye shadow and lip gloss, the Medusas pooled their emergency cash. Misty counted it quickly. "That should be plenty. Wheels for six, coming up. Back in a few," she said breezily. "The usual bet, Mamba?"

"T'ought you'd never ask, girlie. De usual."

Misty disappeared down the road, rolling her pants down around her hips to show off her flat, tanned midriff, her golden hair loose and flowing behind her as she ran.

As they hunkered down to wait, Jeff asked, "What's the bet?"

Karen explained, "Misty has five minutes once she arrives to acquire whatever she's going after. In this case, a car."

Jeff gaped. "Five *minutes?*"

Kat blinked innocently. "What's wrong? That too slow for you?"

He spluttered. "She can't do that in five minutes. She has to buy a drink. Settle in at the bar. Strike up a few conversations. Work her way around to suggesting that she's looking to buy a car. Negotiate a deal. It takes *hours.*"

Kat couldn't resist. She replied blandly, "Is that how a male team does it? How quaint."

Jeff retorted, scowling. "No way can she do it in five minutes."

Aleesha jumped on that lightning fast. "Care to make a side bet, big guy?"

He glanced over at Kat. "Will I lose?"

"Oh, yeah. Bargain for three minutes. Then you might stand a chance."

He shook his head. "This I have to see."

Karen gestured toward the village. "Be our guest. Just don't get caught."

He moved off quickly down the road and disappeared into the night.

Kat felt oddly bereft without him nearby. She was losing her marbles.

Aleesha startled her out of her disgusted musings. "Nice caboose dat boy's sportin'."

Kat replied, grinning. "Shall I tell Michael you said that?"

Aleesha chuckled, dropping the Jamaican accent. "Be my guest. He knows that when I quit looking I'll be dead. He also knows he's got my heart forever."

Kat asked curiously, "How does it work having both a significant other and a job like this?"

Karen crowed. "Oh, ho! Our little Kat does have a crush on Maverick. I knew it!"

Kat scrunched her eyes shut in dismay as Aleesha's motherly arm looped over her shoulder. "'T'ain't nuttin' to be 'shamed of, kitten. He's a fine one, he is."

Kat blinked in surprise. "You approve of him?"

Isabella laughed. "It's not up to us. If you like him, then go get him. I, for one, will be glad to see you happy for a change."

The others nodded. "I'm happy," she declared, a tad defensively.

Karen, the team's tall Marine, and usually one to keep her nose out of others' business surprised her by saying, "No, you're not. You're like I used to be. I was happy to be a Medusa. I was happy to have this job. But I wasn't personally happy. Because I wasn't, I just didn't allow myself to have a personal life. I didn't even know how unhappy I was until Anders came along."

Kat couldn't deny it. Ever since Karen had hooked up with the Norwegian Special Forces officer, she'd been a different woman. These days, she practically glowed from within. Kat muttered, "I don't need to glow, dammit."

"Ahh. Sure ye do. Glowin's good fer a girl," Aleesha replied.

Kat just shook her head. At least they approved of Jeff. That would save her a few hassles, at any rate.

"Speak o' de devil. Here comes Kat's firefly-mon now." Aleesha glanced at her watch and cursed under her breath.

Kat grinned. Aleesha must've lost the bet.

Jeff rejoined them, shaking his head and muttering, "She'll be along in a minute with the van. I've never seen anything like it."

Kat patted his shoulder. "It's all right. We Medusas take a little getting used to."

He glanced up at her, his eyes gleaming. "Now there's an understatement if I ever heard one."

Her pulse jumped. Sheesh. She couldn't even have a

normal conversation with the guy without twittering like a schoolgirl. She really needed to get control of herself.

The sound of an underpowered engine putt-putting up the hill toward them yanked Kat's mind back to the business at hand.

Jeff ordered, "Let's move out, ladies."

As usual, the folks at H.O.T. Watch Ops came through like champs. How they managed to procure a cottage on a secluded beach on the north side of the island at this hour, Jeff had no idea. He rode shotgun and relayed directions from Ops to Misty and her tight T-shirt as she drove them to their ramshackle lodgings.

As hidey holes went, the place wasn't bad. It had running water in the kitchen sink, a flush toilet, and most importantly, electricity and a computer. The desktop model was several years out of date, but it had a CD-DVD drive, and that was what they needed to read the disk the Ghost had given Kat.

In short order after they arrived, the team gathered around the computer, watching it boot up at snail speed. Kat held out a cardboard CD sleeve to him. He took it, examining it closely. "What did he say when he gave this to you?"

"Not much. Apparently, it was attached to the back of a painting he stole, and he accidentally took it, too. He said I'd be in extreme danger if anyone found out I have it."

Jeff was inclined to believe the guy. Eventually, the computer spun up the disk and got around to reading its contents. The blinking hourglass on screen was replaced by the last thing he'd ever expected to pop up....

Over his shoulder, Kat inhaled sharply.

Chinese characters.

Jeff glanced up at her. "What does it say?"

"It's the opening menu to a generic video playback program. Click on that character there to play the video." She pointed at the appropriate pictograph.

Unfortunately, to reach his computer screen, she had to lean over his shoulder and practically lay her cheek against his. They both inhaled simultaneously, breathing in each other's scents instinctively. Her feminine essence mixed with the green, fresh smell of the leaves and moss she'd crawled around in tonight. The combination was heady, making his thoughts whirl in a kaleidoscope of flashing impressions.

Misty piped up. "Anybody see a fire extinguisher?"

Kat started, brushing against his back. "That's right," she commented. "You and Greg had to deal with that booby-trapped computer last year. Do you think this is some sort of self-destruct program?"

Misty laughed. "No. I think the sparks flying off you and the good captain are going to set something on fire pretty soon."

Amused, he glanced out of the corner of his eye and saw Kat close her eyes in mortification. He said sympathetically, "It must really suck, having all these nosy women pick apart your private life like this."

Kat groused. "You have no idea."

He chuckled. But his laugh was cut short when a video image suddenly popped up on the computer screen. "Whoa!" he exclaimed. No wonder the Ghost had warned Kat this tape would put her in extreme danger!

Bloody hell.

Chapter 16

Kat leaned forward to peer at the image on the computer screen. It was grainy and shot from an odd angle, as if the camera were mounted high in the corner of the room. A surveillance camera, then. Not surprisingly, a bedroom came into focus. Even less surprisingly, the bed was occupied.

Kat murmured, "Bella, was the focus on that lens just adjusted?"

The team's photo intelligence analyst murmured, "Yes. A live camera operator shot this footage."

Kat's eyebrows shot up. Which meant this little *ménage à trois* was probably a setup. Which meant somebody was out to blackmail this man. Which begged the questions, who was he, and who would benefit by having this guy by the short hairs?

While she pondered those riddles, the camera zoomed in on the bed and its occupants came into plain view. A middle-aged man, reasonably fit for his age, but his skin loosening and his belly going to paunch, was cavorting with two young, naked men. Who *was* that?

The target of this little cinematic project turned his head momentarily. The camera caught a clear image of him, and Isabella sucked in a sharp breath.

Jeff murmured, "You know him?"

Isabella answered grimly, "That's the Russian oil minister."

Kat's jaw sagged. The Russians might be entirely used to their government officials jumping in and out of the sack with women and turn a blind eye to it. But men with men? Her impression of Russian society was that it was not nearly so tolerant of that. Her thoughts leaped to the next obvious question. Who took the video? And what did they want from the Russian oil minister?

Jeff asked Isabella, "Can you tell anything from this video about who filmed it?"

"I'd need more sophisticated equipment than this. We'll need to send the disk to our analysts for that. My first guess is that it's not Russian. Frankly, their surveillance film quality is better than this."

Kat snorted mentally. The benefit of a long and distinguished history of spying on one's own people, apparently. Aloud, she said, "The next question is who were those guys chasing The Ghost? Is it a safe assumption that they were after this disk? If so, why do they want it?"

"Who are the possible players?" Jeff asked her.

Kat shrugged. "The Chinese might have filmed this and want it back. The Russians could be after it on behalf of Romeo, there. Or some other player may want to get their hooks into the Russian oil minister."

Jeff huffed in disgust. "So we really don't know a whole lot more than we did a few hours ago."

Kat shrugged. "Sure we do. We know that CD was in the possession of someone the Ghost burglarized here on Barbados.

That's a list of only seven suspects. We know that once word got out that the disk had surfaced, a heavy hitter entered the scene fast to try to get his hands on it. Finally, we know the Ghost wanted to dump the disk—in particular to the U.S. government. The Ghost was obviously worried about what the last owner of the disk was going to do with it, which implies that an enemy of the U.S. had the disk until the Ghost took it."

Jeff grinned at her. Even though his voice was teasing, the expression in his eyes was intimate. Personal. "That's why I love you. You're smart *and* optimistic."

L-love? She gulped and had to use all her skill to disguise the shock coursing through her. Surely he'd said that purely in jest. He'd *sounded* like he was joking around, at any rate.

She managed to respond lightly, "Gee, and here I thought you were captivated by my tree-climbing skills."

He laughed. "That, too. You've got to show me how you did that trick of running up the tree trunk sideways sometime."

She winced. He'd seen that, had he? That was exactly the sort of move she didn't like to advertise that she knew how to do. If Uncle Sam found out, she'd be stuck teaching ninja wannabes for the rest of her life. And not only would that drive her crazy, it would go against everything Hidoshi had ever taught her.

Jeff dug out his cell phone. She listened to his call with unabashed curiosity. "Raven, it's Maverick. Just the lady I wanted to talk to. There's been a development."

In short order, Jeff had asked Jennifer and company back at the Bat Cave to do thorough background checks on all the victims of the Ghost's robberies on Barbados. Why would one of them have a blackmail video of the Russian oil minister?

Aleesha commented, "I could get used to having a bunch like the H.O.T. Watch backing me up. They do the drudge work pushing paper while we're out here having all the fun."

Jeff nodded. "I can't tell you how handy they are. They've saved my neck a dozen times and every mission runs smoother with their eyes and ears on my team. Of course, you ladies don't seem to do too badly for yourselves." He threw a sour glance over at Misty.

Kat grinned. "Speaking of which, can I have my shirt back? I'm tired of swimming around in this sack you call clothing, Sidewinder."

Misty quipped, "You're just jealous of the girls." Then her voice dropped into a more serious vein. "I didn't ask for them, you know. They were added when I was still out cold from the accident."

Misty had been in a horrendous car wreck as a teenager and her mother had decided that during the reconstructive surgeries to follow that Misty should be turned into a walking Barbie doll. Her looks were actually a real sore point with her.

Karen commented idly, "Too bad we can't just ask the Ghost where he got the CD."

Kat lurched, her mind racing.

She caught Jeff's intent gaze upon her and he leaned forward. "Talk to me, Kat."

"Is it a good bet that, given enough time, the powers that be at H.O.T. Watch will figure out which of the Ghost's victims would've had a use for, or connection to, that CD?"

Jeff nodded. "They're very good at what they do."

"But knowing that might not account for the guys who jumped us in the gully, right?"

Jeff nodded again.

Kat continued thinking aloud. "We have to assume our commandos reported back to whomever they're working for. Worst case, even more thugs get sent in to help get the disk. The good news is they have no idea who we are and no obvious means of tracking us if we've done our job correctly to erase our tracks tonight. But the hostiles do have one link to that CD whom they can possibly track."

"The Ghost," Jeff said. "But surely after tonight, he's run for the hills. He's probably already off the island."

Kat shrugged. "You're most likely right. He didn't strike me as having a death wish. Otherwise he wouldn't have taken such precautions when he met me. But our hostiles don't know that for sure any more than we do."

Jeff asked, "What do you suggest we do about it?"

Kat leaned forward eagerly. Suddenly it was as clear as a bell to her what her subconscious had been reaching toward. "We know of two more paintings that the Ghost was likely to steal—that last two from that catalog here on Barbados. What if I impersonate the Ghost and steal one of them? You guys can set up a trap around me and I'll act as bait. We'll draw out the hostiles and grab them."

Jeff's look was one of pure horror. "Absolutely not!"

Shocked at his response, Kat stared at him. "Why not? It's a brilliant plan."

"It's too dangerous."

She rolled her eyes. "Oh, come on. I'm a Special Forces operative. How is it too dangerous? I do stuff more dangerous than that all the time."

"You're setting yourself up as bait for a force of unknown size and skill. It'd be a crapshoot. They might come in with six guys like before, or maybe they'll come in with twenty."

"That's what I have the Medusas and H.O.T. Watch for. You all can take care of anything they throw at me."

Jeff glanced around and a look of chagrin came over his face. Kat looked up to see that her teammates were riveted on the exchange between them. Crud.

"Take a walk with me," he ordered tersely.

She concurred wholeheartedly with his impulse to finish this discussion in private. "By all means," she retorted.

Aleesha warned quietly, "Don't get so wrapped up in fighting with each other that you drop your guard. A team of killers is floating around out there who'd love to get their hands on Kat."

Mamba's warning checked Kat's irritation in midstride. Aleesha was right. And the woman should know—she'd fallen in love in the middle of an op, too. Too? *Too?* Kat jolted sharply. There was no *too* about it. She had not fallen in love with Jeff!

He seemed to take Mamba's warning to heart as well, for he paused just outside the cabin to let his eyesight adjust to the dark and to take a long look at the surrounding foliage before heading down the narrow, sandy path to the beach.

She stomped along as best she could beside him. Unfortunately, the soft sand didn't make for good angry stomping. He walked until they'd reached a cove mostly surrounded by cliffs that funneled the waves into crashing surf here. More to the point, the surf was extremely loud. Someone three feet away wouldn't be able to hear them.

He turned sharply to face her. "Don't do this to me, Kat."

"Do what?"

"Don't make me choose between my head and my heart."

"What are you talking about?"

"I can't send the woman I'm planning to marry into a death trap. You may be a ninja to your core, but bone deep, I'm old-fashioned. Hell, a chauvinist, if you will. I can't send a woman I care about into danger."

"Oh, puh-lease. You of all people know I'm not some helpless little thing. I can take care of myself."

"You're not Wonder Woman, dammit!"

"You're right, I'm not. I'm real. I can do stuff Wonder Woman's creators never dreamed of…except for the invisible jet, of course."

"Don't joke around about this," he retorted raggedly.

She peered at him in the faint starlight. He was really worried about her! "Jeff, I appreciate your concern, but I'll be okay. I've got a heck of a good team to back me up. We won't get taken by surprise."

He threw his hands up in the air in frustration.

She tried again. "If I were one of your men and I'd volunteered to do this job, would you have a problem with it? Is my idea operationally sound?"

His gaze narrowed. Reluctantly he answered, "It's a little on the risky side, but yeah, I'd give it serious consideration."

She glared at him reprovingly.

"Okay, so I'd go with the idea if you were one of my guys. And yes, I understand that if I'd let one of them do it, I'm supposed to let you do it, too."

"But…" she asked leadingly.

"But…" He took a quick step toward her and swept her up in his arms. He kissed her with such passion that her toes curled into the cool, damp sand, and her knees went suspiciously weak. Ho-lee cow. Their tongues tangled, mouths slanting across one another hungrily, as they strained closer to one another, pressing body to body from shoulders to ankles.

Eventually, he tore his mouth away from hers. "Can you honestly tell me you feel nothing when we kiss like that?" he demanded.

Panting, she managed to answer, "No, I can't. When you kiss me like that, my world tilts on its axis. I've never pretended otherwise. But that doesn't have anything to do with my doing this job."

"It has everything to do with it, dammit!"

"Why? Male operators expect their wives to wait patiently at home while they put their lives on the line and not to question their judgment out in the field. Why can't I, as a female operator, expect the same of you?"

He shook his head. "I guess I'm not as strong as you. I'd be a wreck, waiting at home while you ran around out here playing superhero. Is that what you want to hear me say? That you're stronger and tougher emotionally than me?"

She couldn't help smiling sardonically. "All women who wait at home for men who do dangerous jobs know *they're* the strong ones. But Jeff, if you want me, if you're going to have me for your girlfriend or wife or whatever, you have to accept this part of me, too. My job involves taking risks, and you're going to have to let me do that. I've trained my whole life to do this, and I'm not walking away from it now. Not even for you."

"Then you admit that you feel something for me?"

She stared up at him in surprise. "Of course I feel something for you. I feel a lot for you!"

"Show me."

"Here? Now?"

"Right here. Right now."

For once, she didn't feel like shying away from his challenge. She was just mad enough to grab the bull by the horns. She dragged her shirt over her head defiantly and threw it down on the sand. He stared, speechless, at her bare breasts. She gave him a moment to take that in, and then she yanked off her belt and flung off her pants and underwear. She was already barefoot, and it was a quick thing to pull out the rubber band holding her hair and shake it loose around her shoulders and breasts. The wind blew cool air upon her naked skin, and the night caressed her damply. The waves pounded wild and free, calling to the siren within her.

"Here I am, Jeff. If you want me, I'm yours. But you have to take all of me—the good with the bad. The whole package."

He gaped for a moment more, and then all of a sudden was fumbling frantically, yanking off his clothes in clumsy haste. "You're magnificent," he breathed.

And then his mouth was on hers, his hands on her body, drawing her down with him to the sand, cushioning her body with his. She stretched out at full length upon him, and the sensation of his body cradling hers all but made her pass out.

"I've wanted you since the moment we met," she mumbled.

He laughed against her lips, his hands busy as he cajoled

her body to a fever pitch of need with hands and mouth and delicious friction of skin on skin. "I thought you hated my guts when we met," he mumbled back.

She kissed her way down his neck to the hollow over his collarbone, gasping at the way his thigh rubbed between her legs. "I loved it when you called me baby. Nobody ever calls me things like that."

"Why the hell not?" he asked as his fingers dipped into the crevice at the base of her spine and all but made her jump out of her skin at the melting lust that shot through her. "You're a sexpot. Men must hit on you all the time."

That made her laugh, her nose buried against his chest. "Not hardly."

"Must be that I'll-break-your-neck-if-you-touch-me vibe you put out." And then his hand slid down her belly and touched her in ways that made her want to sob in pleasure.

Gasping as she arched into his hand, she managed to reply, "But that vibe didn't stop you."

He grinned, looking deeply into her eyes. "I was a goner before you even dropped me in the gym. I took one look and I knew I had to have you."

She cried out as his finger stroked across her moist heat and swollen flesh.

"So responsive," he muttered. "How could anybody miss how sensual you are?"

That startled her. Sensual? Her? She'd never attached that adjective to herself. But as Jeff played her body like a fine instrument, she couldn't argue with him.

His big, warm hands gripped her hips, guiding her down onto him. His heat and size were iron hard and pulsed deep within her, erasing any remaining semblance of organized thought. As her control shattered utterly, her cry of unfettered pleasure rose to mingle with the crashing waves.

She rode him with abandon, matching the rolling rhythm of the ocean, embracing its grandeur and power, letting it wash through her and direct her movements as she gave herself over completely to the moment. She reveled in driving them both deeper and deeper into the night, in letting go of everything—opening the floodgates of her emotions and letting them gush over the dam of her training, her control, her entire being.

Everything she'd ever been was washed away as this new being of pure sensation was being revealed within her. She flung her head back, keening a cry of ecstasy as her first-ever climax burst over her without warning. It electrified her in a blinding shower of tingling sparks, streaking through her like chain lightning, ripping her apart with its power, sending bits of her flying in a thousand different directions.

Jeff rolled over then, pressing her deep into the warm sand as she shuddered around his length and steely power. He took over the rhythm of the ocean and the night, finding her pace and matching it with unerring accuracy. He invaded her very core, now slamming fast and hard, now stroking with aching slowness, until she climbed his chest, clawing him urgently as yet another explosion built, even more powerful than the first one.

"Sing for me, baby," he crooned.

And sing she did. Her legs wrapped around his hips, pulling him even deeper within her as she surged beneath him in total abandon. Their love was a wild thing, bigger than the two of them, bigger than the ocean behind them, bigger than the entire universe, forcing them both to surrender to it completely.

And in that final moment, when they both let go together, they exploded as one, overtaken by an instant of such perfection it stole their breath away. They gazed deep into each other's eyes in wonder as pleasure rolled over both of them, all but ripping consciousness away from them.

Kat descended back into herself slowly. She became aware of Jeff's sand-covered shoulder pressed against her cheek.

She reached up languidly to loop her arms around his neck while he pressed himself up onto his elbows to stare down at her.

"Holy Mother," he murmured in awe.

She smiled up at him tentatively. "No regrets, then? All of me, for better or worse?"

His mouth curved up into a devilish smile. "In sickness and health, until death do us part, darlin'."

She rolled her eyes. "Don't you think you're rushing things just a bit? We've known each other a grand total of three days. Even I'm not insane enough to leap into marriage on that short a courtship."

Of course, if she'd stayed in Korea, she might very well have entered into an arranged marriage whereby she would never have seen the groom, let alone spoken to him before the wedding. Had he lived another few years until she was old enough to marry, she suspected Hidoshi would have been just that old school about it. He'd have married her off into one of the handful of remaining ninja clans. What would he have thought of Jeff? After all, Jeff was a highly trained warrior in the modern tradition. Hidoshi might have found it an interesting match—the meshing of old and new.

Jeff rolled over, drawing her on top of him. He grinned up at her. "You're right. Three days is too soon. I'll give it a full week. After all, I'm patient. But even you understand that this is a done deal between us. Right?"

A done deal? Was she ready to admit that? The reality of the naked man sprawled beneath her was hard to ignore. But it was a complete departure from anything she'd ever even remotely envisioned for her life. Was she ready to abandon a lifetime of solitude and monkish asceticism to embrace this new and foreign world of emotion and passion and impulsiveness?

Kat had no idea how to answer Jeff's question. What he was asking of her was huge. Life changing. She'd always con-

sidered herself to be courageous, but at this exact moment,
she was scared to death. She was standing on the edge of a
cliff. Once she stepped off it, there would be no going back.
Jeff would sweep her into a new life with him and there'd be
no fighting the power of his overwhelming determination to
make her his once she gave into it. Such was the promise—
and the danger—of Cupid's Bolt.

Suddenly, something moved abruptly a few feet away. Her
discarded jeans wiggled slightly and made a faint buzzing
sound. Jeff whipped her over on her back, covering her body
protectively with his from this new threat.

"I highly doubt my cell phone is going to assassinate me,"
she commented wryly.

"Your—" Jeff sagged on top of her. "Being around you is
shooting my nerves all to hell."

As he rolled half off her so she could reach for the phone,
she said, "Then relax already. I can take care of myself." Still
smiling up at him, she answered her phone. "Go ahead."

It was Aleesha. "Sorry to interrupt your fight—or maybe
you two are making up by now, and I'm *very* sorry to interrupt that."

Kat blushed fiercely. Thank goodness Aleesha hadn't
sprung that line on her in person! She managed to choke out
casually enough, "What's up?"

"News. We know who the Ghost stole the disk from. Or
at least we've got a very good idea. I'm afraid you two need
to cut your little tryst short and get back here."

Kat was profoundly relieved that their conversation had
been cut off when it had. Jeff rolled to his feet in a single
powerful move. He was swearing under his breath as he
reached for his discarded clothes—something to the effect of
work having a way of interrupting when a person least needed
or wanted the interruption. Poor guy. The timing really had
sucked from his point of view.

They sprinted back to the cottage, which not only worked

out some of the lingering sexual energy between them, but also shook most of the telltale sand out of their hair and clothes.

Aleesha wasted no time in briefing them when they burst back into the warmth and light of the cottage. "Turns out the Ghost robbed an Indian tycoon's estate a few weeks back."

Kat nodded. She recalled Jeff's summary to her of the robbery.

"This Indian fellow just got our frisky Russian oil minister to agree to sell a whole bunch of oil futures to India that were slated to go to the United States. The folks at H.O.T. Watch say the State Department has been wondering how the Indians pulled off the deal. It was apparently quite a coup for India and a big blow to the U.S."

Jeff interjected. "So, the Indian guy blackmailed the Russian guy. Why was the video in Chinese, then? If the Chinese took the footage, why wouldn't they have used it themselves to blackmail the Russian into selling them the oil?"

Aleesha shrugged. "Could be they got a ton of money by selling the footage. Could be our Indian guy acquired it by doing a private deal of his own. Could be he stole the video. Hard to tell."

Kat interjected. "So we still don't know who the commandos are."

Aleesha nodded. "Correct." She threw an apologetic glance over at Jeff as she continued, "Cobra, I floated your idea of impersonating the Ghost to the gang at H.O.T. Watch Ops."

"And?" Kat asked with ill-disguised interest.

Another apologetic look at Jeff from Aleesha. "They loved the idea. General Wittenauer has already greenlighted the op."

Jeff's jaw went rock hard, and Kat thought she detected a hint of redness around his ears. Without a word, he pivoted stiffly and walked out of the room. The back door slammed. Hard. She might have kept her face still and calm, but she flinched all the way down to the bottom of her soul.

The Medusas looked over at her expectantly.

Aleesha asked gently, "You gonna go after him and talk to him?"

Kat sighed heavily. "It wouldn't do any good. We've both said all we have to say on the matter. He can't stand watching me take risks, and I can't give up what I do or who I am."

Aleesha studied her long and hard—until Kat had to actively clamp down on an urge to squirm. Finally, the Jamaican said, "This op isn't going to be a picnic. You sure you're up for this mission? It's going to take one hundred percent of your focus and concentration."

Kat knew exactly what Aleesha was asking. Was she too emotionally involved with Jeff to give the job her full attention? Kat sighed. Who knew for sure? One thing she did know. She couldn't possibly back out on this mission now and live with herself. She'd drawn her line in the sand with Jeff. He had to accept her career, or there'd be no future for them.

Belatedly, she answered, "I'll be okay. Let's just get on with it."

But in her heart of hearts, she wasn't so sure things were going to be okay at all. She and the Medusas had steamrolled right over Jeff, and he wasn't going to take kindly to that. At the end of the day, he was exactly what he'd said he was— traditional, protective and used to being in charge. It had been too much to ask him to accept her profession—heck, her true identity.

Likewise, she'd made her choice. She was a warrior first and a woman second.

But, God, it hurt to see him go.

Chapter 17

Kat was still awake when Jeff came back to the cottage as dawn broke outside. She'd given up on sleeping soon thereafter and gotten up. He made no effort to speak to her all day. He participated professionally enough in the planning of the night's mission, but when she tried to talk to him in private, she got exactly nowhere with him.

Each time he gave her a closed, stony look—the classic thousand-yard stare of a hardened soldier—her heart broke a little more. By suppertime, she was a complete mess. So much for being able to hold it together no matter what life threw at her.

She went out to the beach where she swayed and stepped through the slow motion dance of an ancient *gigong* ritual designed to calm and center the chi. Twice. It didn't work. She resorted to the more violent Shaolin kung fu forms next. Better. At least working up a good sweat burned off a little of her urge to burst into tears. But she still felt like crap.

"You okay?" Aleesha murmured for at least the tenth time that day as Kat let herself back into the cottage at dusk.

"No, I'm not," she snapped, her fragile calm already wrecked.

Aleesha laughed quietly. "Welcome to the world of wallowing in emotions like the rest of us."

Kat threw her a bitter look. "Yeah, well, it sucks."

"Ahh, but when it's good, it's great, isn't it?"

Kat squeezed her eyes tightly shut. That was just sweat making them burn like that. Just sweat, dammit.

Aleesha sighed. "I really ought to pull you from this mission."

Alarmed, Kat blurted, "You can't. I'm the only one who can do it."

A reluctant nod. "True. But we can postpone it a few days until you're feeling more like yourself."

Kat winced. She was starting to be genuinely afraid that from here on out this *was* herself. How was she supposed to close the floodgates and re-contain all that emotion that Jeff had let out? It would be like trying to empty a lake with a teaspoon.

"I'll be okay, Aleesha. I promise. Once I get into the flow of the mission, my training will take over."

Aleesha looked at her hard. "Make me a promise. If you get in that house and your concentration isn't perfect, you'll call it off and back out."

"But—"

"No buts. Either you promise, or I'm pulling the plug. We'll find some other way to draw these guys out. The way I hear it, those folks in the H.O.T. Watch can do surveillance on the entire island of Barbados at once."

Having seen the Ops center, Kat could believe it. She glanced up to see Aleesha staring at her expectantly.

Kat sighed. "Fine. I promise."

"On your honor?"

"Yes, mother."

Aleesha nodded firmly. "All right, then. Now go take a little rest and we'll wake you up when it's time to go."

* * *

Kat crouched in the bushes outside the mansion that was her target. It was a massive lump of brick and stone, generically Caribbean colonial. And a hell of a tough nut to crack. The place had banklike security, and in the guise of being built hurricane-proof, had also been built practically burglarproof as well.

To the credit of the home's designers, it had taken most of the staff of the H.O.T. Watch, a team at the Pentagon, and several high-powered civilian electronics and security consultants to come up with a way to breach the place. And were it not for the H.O.T. Watch's high-tech satellite systems and an orbiting electronic counterwarfare chopper nearby, she wouldn't have had a prayer of getting inside undetected.

Wherever he was right now, hidden in the trees, was Jeff worried about her? Or was he just mad? Or maybe he felt nothing at all. He certainly seemed to have shut down his emotions earlier. And how ironic was that? She was the one with the legendary self-control while he wore his feelings on his sleeve, and now she was a blithering idiot and he was a rock.

She checked her thoughts sharply. She ought to be reviewing the plan, running it one last time in her head, not to mention keeping an eye out for movement that didn't belong out here. Good thing Aleesha wasn't beside her right now, or this mission would already be over.

Jeff's voice crackled over her earpiece, crisp and emotionless. "H.O.T. Watch and Bravo 51, report when ready." Bravo 51 was the helicopter with the equipment that would jam several electronic portions of the mansion's security system. She didn't hear the chopper yet, but it would move in close when she started her run at the house.

Did he have to sound so cold and uncaring? *Stop that.* He was transmitting on a frequency that close to a hundred people were listening to. How else should he sound?

"You ready, Cobra?" Aleesha prompted.

Kat started. Crud. She was supposed to report when she was ready, and then Jeff would give the green light, and she'd forgotten to do it. Aleesha's transmission had been a subtle kick in the pants to get her head in the game. And Aleesha was right.

Kat slid the switch on her waist pack to hot mike. Everything she said now would broadcast live without her having to press a microphone button. She'd need both hands to do her job pretty soon. "Cobra ready to proceed."

"You are cleared to proceed," Jeff said. "Give us a time hack."

Kat pushed up her sleeve and opened her mouth. The pair of two-inch-long Cyalume sticks she'd tucked into her cheeks emitted a faint glow from between her teeth—enough to see her watch face. "On my mark, it will be 1:30 a.m. Three, two, one, mark."

And with the last syllable, she took off running toward the house. The pressure sensors in the lawn reported wirelessly to the security computer inside, but Bravo 51 had that covered.

On cue, an electronic warfare specialist came up on frequency and announced, "The pressure sensors are jammed. You are clear to cross the grass."

She reached the expanse of green a few seconds later. In her mind, this was the most dangerous part of the mission. She was to run across the lawn in plain view of anyone who might be lurking nearby. After all, the idea was to let the hostiles know she was here. Once she gained the cover of the house, there'd be much less chance to take her out. The working theory was that the commandos would want to capture the Ghost to ask him where the disk was now, and that they wouldn't want to kill him. At least not right away. But if that calculation were wrong, now was the moment they would find out—when bullets slammed into her exposed self.

And then she was across the lawn, crouching in the

shadows of an oleander bush. One of its narrow leaves tickled her nose, and she pushed it aside absently. She had about thirty seconds to wait while Bravo 51 did its magic on the house's outside phone lines. They were going to do something having to do with setting up a feedback loop that blocked a dial tone. The end result would be that when the house's automated alarm system tried to summon the police, no call would get out. At least, that was the plan.

She recognized Jennifer Blackfoot's voice in her ear. "We show no hostile heat signatures on satellite imagery at this time. You are clear to proceed."

"Phones are down," Bravo 51 reported.

That was her signal. She stood up and went to work on the window above her. It was an easy enough matter to cut a foot-wide circle out of the glass and lift it aside. Trickier was the maneuver to use a thin steel rod to manipulate the window latch without breaking the grid of laser beams an inch beyond the window's surface. But with patience and concentration, she got it. After sliding a flat metal strip under the window to maintain contact on the pressure sensors there, she slid the window up gingerly. The house alarms remained silent. Gripping the window frame, she leaped up lightly until she was poised on the narrow sill, balancing on her toes. Carefully, she slipped mirrors into the laser grid until she'd created a gap about ten inches high and eighteen inches wide. It would be a tight squeeze, but that's why she was doing this and not a hulk like Jeff.

The thought of him momentarily broke her breathing rhythm, and she had to pause to remind herself to breathe lightly and evenly. Her calm restored for the moment, she eased through the narrow gap, reaching across a three-foot gap to the back of a leather sofa. Never touching the floor, she slid over the sofa back and twisted to land lightly on its cushioned surface.

"I'm in," she murmured.

The laser grid in here was visible to the naked eye, which made her job of sliding, climbing, leaping and squeezing past it easy. She reached the bookcase beside the door. She commenced pressing, pulling and shifting books in the shelf until she found the dummy book that actually was a switch. It tilted outward from the shelf, and to the right of the library door, a small panel slid open to reveal a numeric keypad.

She described it quickly over her radios. A new voice came up on frequency and didn't identify himself. He did, however, identify the model of alarm system pad she'd described. She spent the next ten minutes following his detailed instructions on how to open the box and disable the alarm.

"Okay, Cobra, give the doorknob a try. If we've done it right, you should be able to open the door and get no alarm siren."

She took a deep breath. Here went nothing. From this moment forward, she'd be on her own inside the house. She turned the cool brass knob slowly. Cracked the door open an inch. Silence. She'd done it.

In point of fact, they expected any bad guys to jump her as she left the house. She ought to be able to proceed from here unhindered. Nonetheless, she eased forward cautiously. It was a short trip down the hall to her right, across the foyer and left into the expansive living room where her target—a magnificent Van der Meer painting—hung.

She eased down the carpeted hall, her passage utterly silent, and frowned. Something didn't feel right. It was nothing she could put her finger on, but an uneasy intuition stole over her. Maybe it was the fact that she was committing a major felony that bugged her.

For no reason she could explain, she paused at the edge of the three-story-high foyer and examined it suspiciously. A huge chandelier dripped with crystal. An ornate table in the middle of the space held a giant Limoges porcelain vase she couldn't wrap her arms around. It was empty at the moment, but would no doubt hold a large floral display when the house was occupied.

The floor was a marble so glossy it glistened like glass in the scant light. Her senses kicked over to another level altogether, her military and martial arts training blending until she was vibrating with awareness at a level so minute her teammates wouldn't believe her if she tried to explain it. And that was probably why she noticed the infinitesimal flicker of movement in a dark shadow under the far leg of the table. She pulled out her sniper scope, a palm-sized telescope she usually used to measure distance to targets. She zoomed it in on the spot where she'd seen the movement.

She frowned. It was a gnat. Lying on its side, one wing beating sporadically in an attempt to free itself. How was the bug trapped? It ought to be able to use its legs to right itself. It was probably just a dying bug and happened to have ended up in that pose. Except...

She sniffed the air experimentally. The faintest odor of something familiar—lightly sweet with a musty undertone— just barely registered. She knew that scent. But where from? She sniffed again, letting its essence flow over her and through her. Summers in Korea. Hidoshi's snug little barn, where the pigs and sheep spent their nights. The paper fly strips that spiraled down from the ceiling, mustard yellow and sticky...and smelling exactly like this.

Flypaper? What did that have to do with this opulent home? Alarm bells went off in her head. Something was not right here. She knelt down to get a better look at that gnat. Now that she thought about it, the gnat was acting just like one of the myriad flies that used to bumble onto Hidoshi's flypaper and then buzz frantically until they died.

The floor. It smelled more strongly of the flypaper glue. From this angle, it looked like a thick layer of polyurethane had been freshly spread over the marble, drying to that glossy sheen. There wasn't a single nick on that satin-smooth surface. What floor had absolutely no nicks or scuffs?

She reached out tentatively to touch the floor and started as it gave way, viscous beneath her touch. She withdrew her hand, and her fingertips stuck to the gooey surface hard enough that she had to yank her hand back, leaving a little skin behind.

That was a powerful epoxy of some kind. The entire floor was coated with glue! Had she stepped in it, she doubted she'd have been able to walk across the floor without sacrificing her shoes, and then her socks, to the glue. Who in their right mind lived in a house like this and poured glue all over their foyer?

A trap.

This was a *trap*.

Adrenaline surged through her veins, screaming its warning at her. She froze, only her gaze roving quickly in all directions. She saw no cameras. No microphones. No other surveillance equipment. Her gut said she wasn't missing anything. The threat she sensed was more human than machine.

Holy sh—

Was she alone in here or not?

Was this why the H.O.T. Watch had seen no hostiles outside? Were they already inside? Was their ambush about to be turned on them? She eased her hand down to her belt and pressed the transmit button three times fast, three times slow, and three times fast, sending out a clicked S.O.S.

Jeff's response was immediate in her ear. "Are you injured?"

Two clicks for no.

"Are you in danger?"

One click for yes.

"Are you under attack?"

How was she to answer that? She wasn't yet, but if there were hostiles in here, she very well could be soon. Did she want the Medusas to come roaring in here with guns blazing, or sneak in and possibly catch whoever else was in the house?

She gave two clicks for no.

"That was a long pause before you answered. Are you about to come under attack?" Jeff asked quickly.

An quick, emphatic single click.

"Do you request backup?"

Again, a single click.

Jeff gave the Medusas a flurry of orders to move in and enter the house through various doors and windows. Jennifer Blackfoot came up on frequency and ordered Bravo 51 to stand by to hit the house with all it had, jamming all electrical function of any kind within the mansion.

And then Jennifer said, "We'll have a Predator drone on sight in two minutes. It's equipped with structure-penetrating radar. Stand by for insertion, Medusas."

Jeff acknowledged her.

Kat hunkered down in the hallway, thinking fast. She couldn't stay here. She was completely exposed and had no cover if this turned into a shoot-out. She glanced around for options. With nothing but the glue-filled foyer before her and an empty hallway behind her, she didn't have much to work with. And then she looked up. Time to use her secret weapon and go vertical. She eased back into a shadow and quickly pulled out her climbing claws, donning them over her shoes and on her hands.

She climbed the hallway wall first, and then eased around the corner into the foyer nearly ten feet up. As soon as she entered the open space, she worked her way higher, crawling up the wall, spiderlike, until she was well above the sight lines of anyone looking from the adjoining rooms into the foyer. She headed for a shadow and awkwardly resumed her game of twenty questions with Jeff.

She laboriously tapped out the Morse code to spell, "Trap. Foyer."

He replied immediately. "Should we avoid the foyer?"

She clicked an affirmative, and he amended Karen's point of entry to the dining-room window instead of the front door.

Kat double-tapped a negative to that. If Karen came into the dining room, she'd have to cross the foyer to get to anywhere but the kitchen.

Jeff understood immediately. "Will it work if Python comes in through the living room?"

Isabella was already scheduled to come in the living room window. That would put two Medusas in there simultaneously. Kat's best guess was that would be where the hostiles would be hiding. They'd surround the painting that the Ghost was after.

Kat clicked a yes to Jeff's suggestion that Karen enter the living room.

Astutely, Jeff asked, "Should I concentrate more force than I already am on the living room?"

She clicked a relieved affirmative.

Yet another adjustment to the entry scheme was made, and all the Medusas were massed outside the windows.

Then Jeff asked, "Where are you now, Cobra? I don't want your teammates shooting you."

She looked down at the foyer. Up here, she'd be clear of any bullets flying into the foyer. She reviewed the house layout quickly in her mind. But if she wanted to join the fight at all, she'd be squarely in her teammates' fields of fire. She had to move.

She tapped out, "Foyer. Moving to living room."

Jeff's response was quick and sharp. "Don't go in there by yourself! Wait for backup!"

He didn't understand where she was at the moment, and although his advice was sound, she needed to ignore it. She sent one last message. "Am on ceiling."

That caused a stir as Jennifer Blackfoot and Aleesha came up simultaneously to ask what the heck she meant by that.

A chuckle was evident in Jeff's voice as he explained. "Cobra straps claws to her feet and hands and can crawl upside down along a ceiling like an insect. Medusas, keep your field of fire at eye level or below and you won't hit her. She'll be overhead when you enter the room."

Jennifer retorted, "Are you kidding?"

Jeff answered, "Nope. I've seen her do it. It's for real."

A male voice interrupted. "The Predator is approaching target. Switching on cameras now. Stand by for real-time photo intelligence analysis."

Kat didn't know if the analyst would be at H.O.T. Watch Ops or sitting on the nearby helicopter, but she didn't care either way, as long as the analyst knew his stuff.

A female voice came up. "I have eyes on target. I show one human heat signature..." A long pause. "Near the ceiling of the foyer, moving down the wall toward the living room entrance."

Jeff murmured, "That is correct. Continue."

"I paint two human signatures in the dining room, one to the right of the foyer entrance, one under the far window."

Bingo. As disconcerting as it was to know she was, indeed, in the middle of an ambush, Kat was relieved to know that her instinct had been right and all this fuss wasn't for naught.

The analyst went on. "I paint four humans in the living room, two on each side of the fireplace on the far wall. I paint one more human in the kitchen—he's on the move, heading toward the butler's pantry."

Kat reviewed the house layout quickly. That guy would be circling through the back side of the house to come into the living room if she had to bet. After all, these guys couldn't use the foyer any more than she could. Misty was slated to come in from that direction. She could drive that guy toward the living room if need be.

The analyst concluded, "That's all. Seven tangos and one friendly doing a Spider-Man."

Jeff came up. "Copy. Medusas, prepare for radio failure. Go on Bravo 51's call of systems activated."

All five Medusas acknowledged in turn, with Kat clicking hers.

Then Jeff said, "Bravo 51, light it up."

"Roger," came the electronic warfare man's voice. "Here we go."

Kat swore she could actually feel the radio waves bombarding her. Static abruptly filled her ears, but she wasn't in a position to turn down her radio volume at the moment. She started crawling, heading for the dining room. Jeff was going to deal with those two guys, and she didn't like those odds. As glass crashed from a half-dozen windows at once and shouting broke out around her, Kat planted a piton at light speed, clicked her rope onto it, and let go of the wall. She swung downward, dropping upside down until her head and shoulders cleared the dining-room entrance. More importantly, her pistol cleared the archway. For tonight's work, she'd chosen a high-caliber handgun with enough stopping power to drop a man. Thankfully, she routinely practiced shooting from odd angles like this, and she took in the scene before her in an instant. Jeff had just crashed through the window and was rolling across the floor while two men in black turned, startled, and were bringing their weapons up to bear on him.

Jeff was situated to nail the guy under the window, so she aimed at the man closest to her, double tapping a pair of shots into the guy before he ever knew she was there. Gunfire erupted from the living room as Jeff efficiently dropped his man. He jumped up and started toward her.

"Stop!" she cried.

He skidded to a halt.

She bit out, "There's epoxy glue all over the foyer floor. You'll have to go around."

He nodded and took off running toward the kitchen.

Quickly, she curled into a ball, caught her rope, and righted herself. She took off, crawling crablike around the foyer toward the shoot-out now in progress in the living room. The space was huge—easily fifty feet square, and crammed with furniture, cabinets, tables, and any manner of good cover. At a glance, all the shooters, both friendly and hostile, looked pinned down and at a stalemate. She glanced over at the doorway Jeff would have to come through. He'd be a sitting duck if he tried to get in there.

She had to do something to tip the scales and fast. He'd be here in a few more seconds.

She climbed up to the twelve-foot-high ceiling and commenced crawling stealthily across it. There. Below her. One of the hostiles. She pulled her pistol and shot down at him, burying a round in the top of his skull and a second round in the back of his neck as he fell.

Her shots elicited a round of gunfire, but none of the hostiles spotted her. She held her position, unmoving. She was completely exposed up here. If any of the bad guys looked up, she was dead meat.

Jeff spun into the room, and the hostiles seemed to realize that the stalemate was breaking against them. They commenced running around, shooting wildly. Although they didn't hit any Medusas, they did effectively foul up everyone's field of fire. Kat saw Aleesha and Isabella draw knives and move out, easing around the perimeters of the space.

Two of the hostiles drew together in the middle of the room, back-to-back behind a giant armoire in a highly defensible position. They were going to be hell to reach. Anyone who came into their line of sight would be shot.

And then she spotted Jeff moving toward them.

He was going to be a hero, dammit.

Swearing under her breath, she scrambled forward. From her vantage point, she saw Jeff pause around the corner from the hostile pair. He shoved a new clip of bullets home and tensed to move. A quick glance showed her the worst. The tango was sighting down the barrel of an AK-47, right at where Jeff was going to emerge, finger poised on the trigger. The second Jeff came around the end of the wet bar, he was going to be blown away.

Desperate to stop him from diving straight into the commando's hail of lead, she scrambled the last few feet. And let go of the ceiling.

Chapter 18

Jeff's heart skipped a beat as Kat's dark shape hurtled down from the ceiling directly in front of where he was about to shoot.

Dear God. Had she been shot?

Pure, unadulterated panic ripped through him, a sick wash of heat that all but knocked his legs out from under him. Roaring in rage and terror, he charged around the corner, heedless of any danger waiting for him. He'd charge the jaws of hell itself for her.

He made out a writhing mass of arms and legs that he dared not shoot at, so he continued to sprint forward, the panic blurring his vision until he could hardly see.

And then a petite figure rose to the top of the pile.

Kat. He'd know her anywhere.

Blindingly fast, she gave a vicious yank. The figure beneath her went limp and thudded to the floor. A second, bigger figure jumped on her from behind, a knife glinting dully in the gloom.

Jeff's weapon swung up to his shoulder. Time ceased, and his mind went to some strange place it had never gone before. A state of suspended animation descended upon him. He became one with the gun, and with the lead slug resting in its depths. He took the shot almost without conscious thought. It was as if his mind directed the bullet's path, guiding its flight unerringly a hair past Kat's temple and into the left eye of her attacker. The guy's head snapped back, and Kat whipped around in his grasp, striking him an open-handed blow that leveled him long before Jeff's bullet dropped him.

As he ran forward toward her, a single thought crossed his mind. He'd never seen another human being move as fast as she just had.

"You okay?" he bit out as they sank to the ground, back-to-back as their attackers had just been.

"Yeah. You?" She panted.

"Fine."

The gunfire in the room was winding down. One more burst of gunfire, he recognized the sound of an MP-7—standard issue for the Medusas—and then it went quiet. The silence was intense after all the shots in an enclosed space, and his ears rang fiercely.

"Report!" he called.

One by one, the Medusas reported in. Misty's voice sounded strained, as if she were injured.

"Mamba," he called.

"I'm on it," the medic replied, already running toward the last sound of Misty's voice.

He stood up cautiously. "Clear the space by standard quadrants. We'll meet at the fireplace."

Kat stood up behind him and it was all he could do not to spin around and snatch her into his arms, to run his hands over her to assure himself that she wasn't hurt. But now was not the time. Not yet.

He methodically checked his portion of the room, verifying that the two hostiles he and Kat had taken out were, indeed, dead. A few minutes later, the team converged by the fireplace, Mamba holding Misty's left arm and still binding a splint into place. For her part, Misty's face was drawn in pain.

"What have you got, Mamba?"

"Bullet in the upper arm, lodged near the bone. Gonna have to dig it out. Bleeding under control. She's ambulatory but not combat capable."

He nodded briskly. It was weird to let a woman suffer with a gunshot wound like this, but if he'd ever doubted it before, he didn't now. These women were soldiers of the first caliber, every bit as good as his own men. They'd worked like a well-oiled machine, in spite of the close confines, the lack of radios and determined resistance by the hostiles.

Kat looked up from the body she'd just searched. "Russian. What do you want to bet our frisky oil minister sent them to get his movie back."

Jeff nodded. "That movie's gonna cost India a big oil contract or a whole lot of egg on that Russian minister's face. The State Department's gonna kiss your feet when you give that disk to them."

Kat made a face. "That's okay. I'll settle for a decent foot massage. No kissing required."

He grinned and spoke off frequency. "It all depends on who's doing the kissing and how. You're gonna like what I do to your toes."

Kat's eyes popped wide open, clearly imagining the possibilities.

The static in his ear stopped abruptly. Hallelujah. In the chaos of battle he hadn't noticed it, but it had really been starting to get on his nerves the last minute or two.

"Say status," Jennifer Blackfoot ordered.

She sounded tense. Which was saying something for her.

He replied, "All hostiles down. One friendly injury. We'll need medevac to a hospital, but it's not life-threatening."

"Well done, Maverick, ladies."

He started. That had been General Wittenauer's voice. He'd had no idea the Old Man had been monitoring this op.

"Let's move out," Jeff ordered.

They headed for the back of the house. Bravo 51 was being directed to move in and pick up Misty and Mamba and fly them back to the H.O.T. Watch cave. Aleesha would remove Misty's bullet in their operating room, where there wouldn't be any awkward questions asked about how Misty'd been shot.

The helicopter lifted off, and the Medusas hiked off through the trees to recover the surveillance gear they'd abandoned when he'd ordered them to rush the house. Kat hung back with him, since she'd carried all her gear with her when she broke in to the mansion.

She gazed up at him in the starlight beseechingly. She did not speak, but then, she didn't have to. Her eyes said everything. She was hurt. Missed him. Wanted to talk to him. Wanted him to understand that this was who she was.

"I—"

A dark shape hurtled out of the trees and barreled into Kat just as a gunshot rang out.

Jeff dived for Kat and the prone figure on top of her. Before he could do a thing to help her, Kat had moved like lightning, slipping the grip of her captor and reversing their positions.

Another shot rang out, and a foot-long divet of grass flew up a scant inch beyond Kat's head. Jeff jumped to his feet, grabbing the attacker by one arm as Kat took him by the other. The three of them sprinted across the lawn, zigzagging for cover.

A French-accented voice panted. "One shooteur. In the woods that way. I show you."

"Ahh. We meet again," Kat answered warmly.

The Ghost? Jeff's jaw dropped as he ran. The guy had literally run right into his grasp? Exultation shot through him.

They dived into a stand of fig trees and the shooter paused for the moment.

"This way!" The Ghost took off crawling on his hands and knees, with Kat in tow.

"You're not going to follow him, are you?" Jeff demanded in a whisper.

"Of course I am."

"You've already walked into one trap tonight. Are you going to dive into another one?" Jeff challenged.

"He just saved my life. He's not a killer." And with that, Kat turned away and rose to a crouch, running after the thief.

Jeff closed his eyes for a moment in sheer exasperation and then gave chase. The pair had paused at the edge of the fig grove. He drew close in time to hear Kat murmur, "Can you point him out from here?

"I t'ink not."

"Use this," she said. Jeff gaped as she pulled out her spotter's scope and passed it to the Frenchman.

"Ahh. There 'e is."

Kat glanced over her shoulder. "Give me your gun, Jeff."

"I'll take the shot—"

She cut him off. "I'm a trained sniper. You're not. I'll take the shot."

Shaking his head, he peeled his MP-7 off his shoulder and handed it over. "It's sighted true. I make corrections manually."

"Perfect." Kat sounded distant, already completely focused on the shot to come. She transmitted over her radio. "Does anybody have the current winds at this location?"

She stretched out on the ground, settling into a prone position, the rifle coming up to her cheek.

Jeff recognized Carter Beigneaux's voice from H.O.T. Watch Ops. "Five knots, variable from heading one hundred to one hundred and thirty."

"Thanks," Kat muttered.

"What's going on?" Jennifer demanded.

Jeff answered, "A stray shooter."

"You need telemetry?" Jennifer blurted in alarm.

"No. Cobra's got it handled. Stand by."

And something deep in his gut really did believe she had the situation under control. He was still and silent behind her as she set up for the shot.

"Where is he?" she murmured to the Ghost.

The Frenchman began to give a description, and after a few seconds, Kat cut in. "Got him."

She murmured, "Target acquired. Request green light."

Jeff answered immediately. "You are greenlighted."

At his feet, she went completely still, as relaxed as if she were deeply asleep. Her legs sprawled wide to stabilize her body on her belly. Her right arm draped over his gun's stock, and her cheek pressed against the housing as gently as a lover. He actually felt the calm that rolled off her, the utter concentration as her entire world narrowed down to a single point in her sights.

She exhaled slowly.

And then a single shot rang out.

Kat spoke emotionlessly. "Clean head shot. Target is down."

Jeff sagged behind her.

She rolled over onto her back and the Ghost helped her to her feet. To the Frenchman, she said, "Thank you, my friend. I owe you one this time."

"No, we are even. You went into that ambush instead of moi. I t'ink I would have died in there."

"Not before you told them where you got that disk of yours," Jeff commented.

The Ghost looked at him in surprise. "The Renoir job."

Jeff nodded. They'd been right. The Indian businessmen. "Do you know who those men waiting for you were?"

"They are Russian. Not government. Private. How you say—mafiosi. The oil minister. He want his movie back and hire them."

"Can you prove that?" Jeff asked.

The Ghost shrugged. "My source… 'e cannot reveal himself to the likes of you. But 'e is never wrong."

Jeff sighed. As he'd expected.

Jennifer spoke into his ear. "Police en route. Those outside shots were heard and reported by a neighbor."

Kat started. "You must leave, my friend. The police are on their way."

Jeff started. "Leave? Not on your life! He's stolen a hundred million dollars' worth of art. He's under arrest!"

Kat turned to him. She didn't say a word. She just looked at him with sad, wise eyes. And he knew in his heart that she was right. The honorable thing to do was as plain as day in her gaze. No wonder Vanessa Blake called her the Medusas' compass arrow of right and wrong. He hesitated a moment more…

And then nodded in acknowledgment.

He turned to face the Ghost. "In light of the fact that you just saved the life of the woman I plan to marry, I think we can make an exception in this case. If you head down toward the beach, we can stall the police here."

A wide smile broke across the thief's face. He bowed his head briefly at Jeff, then turned to face Kat. He pressed a small rectangle of white into her hand. "If you ever have need of me, you have but to call this number. A message will reach me."

He turned to leave, then paused and looked over his shoulder.

"She is a precious diamond, a woman of extraordinary worth. Take good care of her, monsieur."

"Trust me. I plan to. For the rest of my life and hers."

And as the Ghost faded away into the night, Jeff turned to face his future. Kat stepped into his arms eagerly, fitting against him as if she'd been born for him.

"Thank you," she murmured.

"For what? For letting him go? Or for finally seeing you for who you really are, and finally wrapping my brain around the fact that you can handle yourself every bit as well as I can?

Or for accepting you for who you are—all of you, including your job and your crazy training and your blasted sense of honor?"

She laughed quietly. "All of that."

"I love you, you know."

She froze. Slowly she leaned back to look up at him. "Are you sure?"

It was his turn to laugh. "Oh, yeah. I'm sure. I was ready to slay lions and charge into hell for you in there. I'm a goner. Cupid's Bolt did me in."

"Gee, and here I thought it was Medusa's arrow that got you."

"That she did. She's got all of me forever if she'll have me. What do you say, darlin'? Will you marry me?"

Her smile was bright enough to light the heavens and illuminated his heart until he thought it might burst. "I thought you'd never ask. It would be my honor to have you."

Jennifer Blackfoot's voice came up on frequency, startling them both. "Uh, one of you is leaning on your transmit button."

Kat buried her face against his chest in mortification as laughter and cheering erupted over their earpieces. And then General Wittenauer's voice came up on frequency. "You'd better take good care of her, son. She's like a daughter to me."

Jeff closed his eyes in chagrin. "Yes, sir. I will, sir." He gazed down at Kat apologetically. "So much for privacy for the two of us."

"Welcome to my world," she said, rolling her eyes.

He grinned down at her. "I think I'm gonna like it there. A lot." He took her hand in his, and together, the two of them turned to walk into whatever the future held.

* * * * *

*Celebrate 60 years of pure reading pleasure
with Harlequin®!*

To commemorate the event, Harlequin Intrigue® is
thrilled to invite you to the wedding of The Colby
Agency's J. T. Baxley and his bride, Eve Mattson.

That is, of course, if J.T. can find the woman who left
him at the altar. Considering he's a private investigator
for one of the top agencies in the country—the best of
the best—that shouldn't be a problem. The real setback
is that his bride isn't who she appears to be…and her
mysterious past has put them both in danger.

Enjoy an exclusive glimpse of Debra Webb's latest addition to
THE COLBY AGENCY:
ELITE RECONNAISSANCE DIVISION

THE BRIDE'S SECRETS

Available August 2009 from Harlequin Intrigue®.

The dark figures on the dock were still firing. The bullets cutting through the surface of the water without the warning boom of shots told Eve they were using silencers.

That was to her benefit. Silencers decreased the accuracy of every shot and lessened the range.

She grabbed for the rocks. Scrambled through the darkness. Bumped her knee on a boulder. Cursed.

Burrowing into the waist-deep grass, she kept low and crawled forward. Faster. Pushed harder. Needed as much distance as possible.

Shots pinged on the rocks.

J.T. scrambled alongside her.

He was breathing hard.

They had to stay close to the ground until they reached the next row of warehouses. Even though she was relatively certain they were out of range at this point, she wasn't taking any risks. And she wasn't slowing down.

J.T. had to keep up.

The splat of a bullet hitting the ground next to Eve had her rolling left. Maybe they weren't completely out of range.

She bumped J.T. He grunted.

His injured arm. Dammit. She could apologize later.

Half a dozen more yards.

Almost in the clear.

As she reached the cover of the alley between the first two warehouses, she tensed.

Silence.

No pings or splats.

She glanced back at the dock. Deserted.

Time to run.

Her car was parked another block down.

Pushing to her feet, she sprinted forward. The wet bag dragged at her shoulder. She ignored it.

By the time she reached the lot where her car was parked, she had dug the keys from her pocket and hit the fob. Six seconds later, she was behind the wheel. She hit the ignition as J.T. collapsed into the passenger seat. Tires squealed as she spun out of the slot.

"What the hell did you do to me?"

From the corner of her eye she watched him shake his head in an attempt to clear it.

He would be pissed when she told him about the tranquilizer.

She'd needed him cooperative until she formulated a plan. A drug-induced state of unconsciousness had been the fastest and most efficient method to ensure his continued solidarity.

"I can't really talk right now." Eve weaved into the right lane as the street widened to four lanes. What she needed was traffic. It was Saturday night—shouldn't be that difficult to find as soon as they were out of the old warehouse district.

A glance in the rearview mirror warned that their unwanted company had caught up.

Sensing her tension, J.T. turned to peer over his left shoulder.

"I hope you have a plan B."

She shot him a look. "There's always plan G." Then she pulled the Glock out of her waistband.

Cutting the steering wheel left, she slid between two vehicles. Another veer to the right and she'd put several cars between hers and the enemy.

She was betting they wouldn't pull out the firepower in the open like this, but a girl could never be too sure when it came to an unknown enemy.

Deep blending was the way to go.

Two traffic lights ahead, the marquis of a movie theater provided exactly the opportunity she was looking for.

The digital numbers on the dash indicated it was just past midnight. Perfect timing. The late movie would be purging its audience into the crowd of teenagers who liked hanging out in the parking lot.

She took a hard right onto the property that sported a twelve-screen theater, numerous fast-food hot spots and a chain superstore. Speeding across the lot, she selected a lane of parking slots. Pulling in as close to the theater entrance as possible, she shut off the engine and reached for her door.

"Let's go."

Thankfully he didn't argue.

Rounding the hood of her car, she shoved the Glock into her bag, then wrapped her arm around J.T.'s and merged into the crowd.

With her free hand she finger-combed her long hair. It was soaked, as were her clothes. The kids she bumped into noticed, gave her death-ray glares.

They just didn't know.

As she and J.T. moved in closer to the building, she grabbed a baseball cap from an innocent bystander. The crowd made it easy. The kid who owned the cap had made it even easier by stuffing the cap bill-first into his waistband at the small of his back.

Pushing through the loitering crowd, she made her way to the side of the building next to the main entrance. She pushed J.T. against the wall and dropped her bag to the ground. Peeled off her tee and let it fall.

His gaze instantly zeroed in on her breasts, where the cami she wore had glued to her skin like an extra layer. A zing of desire shot through her veins.

Not the time.

With a flick of her wrist, she twisted her hair up and clamped the cap atop the blond mass.

"They're coming," J.T. muttered as he gazed at some point beyond her.

"Yeah, I know." She planted her palms against the wall on either side of him and leaned in. "Keep your eyes open. Let me know when they're inside."

Then she planted her lips on his.

* * * * *

Will J.T. and Eve be caught in the moment?
Or will Eve get the chance to reveal all of her secrets?
Find out in
THE BRIDE'S SECRETS
by Debra Webb.
Available August 2009 from Harlequin Intrigue®.

We'll be spotlighting a different series every month throughout 2009 to celebrate our 60th anniversary.

LOOK FOR
HARLEQUIN INTRIGUE®
IN AUGUST!

To commemorate the event, Harlequin Intrigue® is thrilled to invite you to the wedding of the Colby Agency's J. T. Baxley and his bride, Eve Mattson.

Look for *Colby Agency: Elite Reconnaissance*

THE BRIDE'S SECRETS
BY DEBRA WEBB

Available August 2009

www.eHarlequin.com

You're invited to join our Tell Harlequin Reader Panel!

By joining our new reader panel you will:

- Receive Harlequin® books—they are FREE and yours to keep with no obligation to purchase anything!
- Participate in fun online surveys
- Exchange opinions and ideas with women just like you
- Have a say in our new book ideas and help us publish the best in women's fiction

In addition, you will have a chance to win great prizes and receive special gifts! See Web site for details. Some conditions apply. Space is limited.

To join, visit us at

www.TellHarlequin.com.

REQUEST YOUR FREE BOOKS!

2 FREE NOVELS PLUS 2 FREE GIFTS!

Silhouette® Romantic

SUSPENSE

Sparked by Danger, Fueled by Passion!

Silhouette® Romantic
SUSPENSE

COMING NEXT MONTH

Available July 28, 2009

#1571 CAVANAUGH PRIDE—Marie Ferrarella
Cavanaugh Justice
When detective Julianne White Bear is sent from another town to
help hunt a serial killer, she brings with her a secret motive. Detective
Frank McIntyre has his hands full heading the task force, but he can't
deny his attraction toward Julianne—and the feeling is mutual. They're
determined to put romance on hold until justice is served, but it isn't
always that easy....

#1572 HER 24-HOUR PROTECTOR—Loreth Anne White
Love in 60 Seconds
FBI agent Lex Duncan and casino heiress Jenna Rothchild play each othe
from the moment they meet. Even as the heat between the two sizzles
hotter than the Las Vegas desert, danger intensifies around them. Suddenly
Lex becomes the one man who can rescue the sexy young heiress…in
more ways than one.

#1573 HIS PERSONAL MISSION—Justine Davis
Redstone, Incorporated
Ryan Barton's teenage sister is missing, and his only hope to find her is
Sasha Tereschenko—the woman he'd loved and lost two years ago. Family
is everything to Sasha, who leaps into action. While the two track down th
predator possibly holding Ryan's sister, their former attraction arises again
and their lives—and hearts—are put at risk.

#1574 SILENT WATCH—Elle Kennedy
Samantha Dawson has been in hiding since the night of her brutal attack.
Now, living in isolation under a new identity, she is surprised to find a sex
FBI agent on her doorstep. Blake Corwin promises to protect Samantha i
exchange for her help with her attacker's latest victim. But the last thing h
expected was to fall for Sam, and when she again becomes a target, Blake
will do anything to save her.

SRSCNMBPA0709